Crime & Mystery Short Stories

An Anthology of Short-Read Thrillers and ⁙⁙

By Daphne Ha

Table of Contents

Part of the Gang

Chapter 1: Those Sunglasses

Sirens pass by Jamie's home. He hates the noises. They wake him up. He has been sleeping in for the past week or so. He gradually extends his arms and legs, scratches his head, and looks around him with his eyes half closed.

" Aaarghh ... too early," he says as he drops on his back and drops off to sleep again.
Weee-o-wee-o-wee-o-weee!

" Annoying sirens," he grumbles after he awakens again, putting the pillow on his head to rock the sounds.

Weee-o-wee-o-wee-o-weee!

" Fine! I'm up! There's no point in trying to sleep anyway."

He looks around him. It's pitch black, since the curtains are closed. He sits up, gazes in front of him for a few minutes, and stands. He walks to the window and opens the curtains.

" Ah! Too bright!" he complains.

Jamie then decides to open them just a little, so that the sunshine shines through the thin opening.

Jamie does not have much. He resides in the run-down neighborhoods and has been searching for a great job for a long time. It hasn't gone well yet; unemployment is everywhere. No one appears to find a good job in this city.

" Time to make another attempt," he says as he sighs.

He walks to his closet and puts on his suit ... his only suit, the one he utilizes for job interviews. He knows it will impress his potential employer if he looks classy, even when he does not live like a classy resident. It's really about the look, about status. But despite his efforts to stand out and look proficient, he hasn't succeeded; he hasn't been hired, and paying his rent has become a drag.

" Looking good," he tells himself as he looks in the mirror before heading out the door.

He walks across the street, crosses another one, and turns left twice. There it is: The job company. He approaches the door, opens it, and steps inside.

" Good day, sir. What can I do for you?" the woman behind the desk asks.

" I'm still looking for a job," Jamie says.

" That's great because we just got a new task from the police."

" The police? What type of task is it?"

" They wouldn't say, but they asked me to let them know as soon as I would find anybody trying to find a job. Shall I contact them and ask and let them know you are here?"

" Sure. That sounds great," Jamie says.

Several minutes after that, Jamie has a time and area for a consultation at the police headquarters. He decides to walk there. He has all the time in the world anyway. Traffic was pretty bad. There were automobiles and semi-trucks everywhere. A few times, he takes extra care when crossing the street. He witnesses a mishap and a traffic collision. What a filthy city this has become! Well ... not totally ... some people reside in the wealthy parts, neighborhoods with large properties, gorgeous gardens, and swimming pools in the yards. It would be excellent to live there, he thought.

He sees the police station. It's right in front of him. After a few minutes walking and a long, red stop light, he goes into the structure. At the front desk, someone guides him to a closed space on the other side of the police headquarters. It's a dark room with a huge mirror in it. Jamie figures it is probably one of those mirrors which is actually a window, so that people on the other side can see him although he cannot see them.

" So, your name is Jamie?" a man asks as he walks in.

" That's correct, sir," Jamie says.

" And you are here for the new job?"

" I am."

" Excellent. Have a seat. I will clarify your job description. My name is trivial. This police mission is classified, and I will ask you some questions before we start, just to ensure you are qualified for the job."

" Sounds fair," Jamie says.

The man questions him for twenty minutes and after that decides to unfold the secret information about the job. He takes another twenty minutes to describe all the details and then ends his story.

" We specifically had the job company make it appear as a normal job," the man says. "Considering the nature of the task, it could only be done by a civilian, not a law enforcement officer. You understand that, don't you?"

" Clear as glass, sir," Jamie replies.

" Then you are prepared. I will see you some other time, Jamie. Don't forget that this information is of the utmost significance. It's top secret. You cannot reveal it to anybody."

With those words they bids him farewell. Jamie walks directly to a street behind the biggest apartment buildings and businesses in the city, a street known for its dark past and filthy trades. He knows what he has to do. It isn't a common, daily assignment. This is serious stuff. He feels honored that the policeman entrusted him with this. Unexpectedly, he hears a voice.

" Hey, pssst ..."

He looks behind him. He sees a guy in jeans and a black shirt, holding a bag and wearing sunglasses. He looks like he intends nothing good, but for some reason, Jamie doesn't feel threatened by him at all.

" Wan-na make some additional money? You appear like a smart guy. My name is Devon. I know a way to score big with the big boys."

Jamie is curious.

" Go ahead and tell me. I'm listening."

" So I work for a company that ... well ... never mind the name. It's a company with powerful leaders. They are willing to pay you well. Sound good?"

" Of course," Jamie says.

" Okay, follow me."

Jamie follows the shady figure into another street. They crisscross through the labyrinth of unknown back alleys in the heart of the city. After several turns, the guy with the black shirt says, "Wait here."

Jamie does what he says. He watches as Devon walks through a door and listens to him talking about something with one of his colleagues. He can't figure out what they are saying, but he concludes it's probably about him doing a job for them.

Sometime later, the guy in the black shirt comes out.

" You're good," he says. "Are you prepared to hear what you need to do?"

" Yes," Jamie answers.

They go into the room and a huge guy stands in front of him behind a desk. He is wearing a white shirt and a tie.

" Do you appreciate the law?" he asks.

" That depends," Jamie says.

" On what?"

" On whether there is something in it for me."

" Good," the huge guy says. "My name is Alexander. I am the brains in this operation. I expect my man here told you that you would get your hands dirty when working with us."

" Yes he has, and I have no problems with that."

" If you did, we 'd need to show you the door. As our coworker, you are obligated to swear secrecy. You will perform jobs on a commission basis. When you're done with the job, you report to me. Understood?"

" Yes, sir."

" All right," Alexander says. "Then it's time to tell you what you need to do, but first, take these sunglasses. They're a present from our boss."

Chapter 2: The Tax System

Alexander offers Jamie some sunglasses. They look expensive. Jamie accepts them happily, realizing that even if he sold just this pair, he would probably have the ability to pay the rent for a month.

" How much did you say these were?" Jamie asks.

" Oh, those are about 600 dollars," Alexander says. "Consider it a down payment. For what you're about to do, we will make enough money to purchase hundreds of pairs like that."

" And ... the boss? Where is he at? If you tell me, I can personally look him up and thank him for his generous gift."

" Don't inquire about the boss!" Alexander screams. "You have not proven yourself to be trustworthy enough to ask such questions. He won't see anyone he does not trust."

" No worries," Jamie says. "Can you show me what to do?"

" Okay, listen carefully," Alexander says. "I am only going to explain this once. See this photo?" he asks, pointing at a photo on the wall. "That's Mr. Gregor. He is the tax collector of the city. Conceited wealthy guy, if you ask me. Anyway, he thought it was fun to tax us on our businesses."

" What type of businesses?" Jamie asks.

" Never mind that. He just did. He wrote us a letter, specifying that we owe the federal government 2 million dollars in taxes. It's ridiculous, I know. Why would truthful people like us try to prevent ourselves from paying taxes? I do not know where all these accusations come from, but we are going to do something about it, and you will play an important part in that operation."

" What do I need to do?" Jamie asks.

Alexander grabs a map from the drawer in the corner of the room.

" This is the tax workplace in the city structure. That, there, is the main workplace where this guy goes every morning. Mr. Gregor is a scatterbrain. He needs to remain in his routine or he will lose sight of what is happening that day. I am sure this is why they hired him: So stuck on rules and numbers that he is all in the details and does not see what's going on around him. At 9:30 a.m., he gets his early morning drink from the coffee machine in the corridor. It's most likely some soup or hot chocolate; I don't care. The video cameras don't lie. After he takes his drink, he heads to his office, but he needs to head through a series of cubicles with computer systems and paperwork. That's where you come in. Tomorrow is the day he will take our tax documents to his office ..."

After Alexander's clarification of Mr. Gregor's early morning routine, the trio gets on the computer, prepares the essential documents, and gets everything prepared to break the tax collector's regimen in the early morning.

Jamie isn't too happy with what he needs to do to get these people's trust, but he knows that paying the bills is essential too. He goes to sleep and drops off to sleep fast.

The next morning, the adventure begins. Jamie is a little anxious but positive that he can pull it off.

They meet in front of the tax office complex at 8:00 a.m. Jamie is fidgeting. He hasn't done anything like this before.

" So you go to the hallway," he tells Devon. "And you, Jamie, will be all set when I spill my hot chocolate on Mr. Gregor's t-shirt. You will only have a few seconds. Do not dissatisfy me."

" I will not," Jamie says.

They go different ways. Jamie heads to the workplace and hides a little between the cubicles of the federal government employees. He has a stack of documentation in his hands. Now it's only a matter of time before he can change the papers.

Devon is in the hallway. He pretends to eat a sandwich and take a look at some phony papers he brought as a distraction.

Devon waits ... and waits ...

There is Mr. Gregor. As always, he heads straight for the coffee machine, looking at his watch and putting his papers on the right side.

" That's a fascinating tie," Devon says as he approaches him and stands on his left side.

" What? Oh yes, I got it a few months ago. I love the patterns," Mr. Gregor says.

" Well, I think it stands apart, but not as much as his tie."

Devon points to a colleague on the right side. Mr. Gregor looks and does not see that when his head is turned, Devon puts a little hypnotic powder in his tea. Mr. Gregor turns his head back and stares at Devon as if there is something suspicious about him. Devon smiles.

" Did you see him?" Devon asks.

" Uhm ... no. Who were you pointing at?" Mr. Gregor asks.

" Oh, he must have left the room right before you saw him. I would check him out sometime today. His tie is fantastic too. You guys ought to do a contest. Anyway, I am pretty hectic. I got ta go. See you later."

" Odd duck," Mr. Gregor mumbles.

He takes his tea and documents and walks through the other workplaces to his own. Right at that moment, Alexander walks into him.

BAF!

" Oh, excuse me," Alexander says as he accidentally (or actually on purpose) spills his hot drink on Mr. Gregor. Startled by this abrupt encounter, Mr. Gregor drops his papers. That's when Jamie crawls over the floor and begins gathering the papers.

" Oh, in the future, could you please watch out where you're going?" Mr. Gregor asks with irritation in his voice. "Now I have to get a rag and clean my shirt."

In the meantime, Jamie skims through Mr. Gregor's paperwork and exchanges his own papers for his. He picks them up, puts Mr. Gregor's original paper beneath his shirt and hands them over to Mr. Gregor.

" Thank you, man. At least some people here have manners."

With those remarks, Mr. Gregor retires to his workplace and takes a seat, whipping off the spilt drink.

" Did you get them?" Alexander whispers.

" Yes, let's get out of here," Jamie whispers back.

Together, they go to a different room and put the documents on the desk. They don't have much time. Mr. Gregor will take a sip of his drink, drop off to sleep for about 15 minutes and perhaps see that the papers are different. Alexander and Jamie look at the signature on the papers, copy and paste some information, modify a few details, and stack them up before leaving the room.

" There," Alexander whispers. "See? He's asleep. Tread carefully. You must not wake him up."

Jamie casually walks past the other colleagues and after that sneaks into Mr. Gregor's office. One foot after the other, he slowly approaches his desk and exchanges the original, modified papers for the ones he offered Mr. Gregor to make it appear like everything was regular. He looks behind him, checks one more time if he is still asleep, and then follows the other two bad guys outside.

" You did it!" Alexander says enthusiastically. "Now you are all set for another job, but first your payment."

He writes Jamie a check with an amount of money Jamie had never imagined getting. This was good business. It may not have been entirely proper or legal, but if he could make this much for each job he carries out, he would be a millionaire in no time. Jamie smiles. He recognizes the magnitude of this criminal organization, but there is more, and he is about to learn what that is.

The next day, Jamie arrives at the same building where he met Alexander. He knocks, gets let it, and waits on his next assignment.

" As you might have heard ..." Alexander begins, "... we belong to the biggest underground organization in the city. It's called Counter, and you have the honor to work for them. I have been a Counter member for years now and I can guarantee you that you will face a life full of high-end stuff if you follow our orders and do not question them."

" I've heard of it, and I am honored," Jamie says.

" Then let me give you your next assignment," Alexander continues. "The harbor isn't a safe place any longer. We used to be able to do what we wanted, but now, the authorities are all over it. They put guards there and are continuously watching the transportation services. You mentioned earlier that you've had some fight training, right?"

" That's correct."

" Well, if you could get the guards on the evening of the 26th, then we can finally import our ... uhm ... product."

" Sure. No worries. Uhm... how many guards are we talking about?"

" Usually about eight or nine. Like I said, it's not going to be easy," Alexander says.

" I'll find a way," Jamie says.

Before he realizes it, the days on the calendar fly by and the 26th is at the door. Jamie puts on a black jacket to be less conspicuous and blend into the darkness of the night. He leaves his costly sunglasses at home.

He has a plan.

He has figured out a way to take this handful of guards down.

He goes to the docks. The windy sea and moon are perfect distractions for his attacks. Sneaking behind the large containers, he looks at any patterns of the guards' habits and movements. He uses some binoculars to count their steps and come up with a strategy.

The containers are the solution.

Suddenly, he bangs on one of the containers.

BANG! BANG! BANG! BANG!

The guards turn around.

" What was that?" one of them asks.

" It seemed like it came from over there," another one says. "Let's go check it out."

All the guards go the same way. They walk to the containers where Jamie was banging to make sounds. They are shocked when they see that one of the containers has been opened. Curious to see what's inside, they walk into the container.

BAM!

Jamie shuts the door and locks it.

" That was simple," he says. "Not extremely reliable guards if you ask me."

He whistles to the other side of the docks.

" It's alright! The coast is clear!" he says.

" Hey! Let us out!" the guards are shouting from inside the container.

" Oh, be quiet," Jamie says as he leaves.

He meets Alexander and Devon next to the containers.

" Thanks, Jamie. Now we can take our goods out of the ship. Could you give us a hand?"

" Sure," Jamie says.

Following them, they go up a wooden plank and see the five men transporting away huge boxes. Jamie does not question anybody and just begins helping them, lifting a box here, and putting down another one there. The boxes aren't heavy, but according to Alexander, they are very important.

But then, Devon drops one of the boxes. It moves open and a lot of hundred dollar bills fall out.

" Clumsy imbecile," Alexander sneers. "Put those things back in the box immediately."

As Devon picks up the dollar bills, Jamie is starting to see what is happening here. The dollar bills are fake. It's fake money that they printed without the government's approval. It's easy to see, since a few of them are lacking a few complicated artistic patterns you generally see on real one hundred dollar bills.

" Finish the job, and you'll get a share of it," Alexander says as he smiles. "Of the real ones, I mean."

Chapter 4: Theft of the Best

Back at Alexander's workplace, Jamie sits down and gazes at the computer. He is in the gang now. He is in. He has shown himself to be trustworthy. There is no turning back. He might as well keep going with all this criminal stuff.

Alexander walks in after he returns from the restroom.

" Jamie," he begins, "you have done your duty and offered us an exceptional service. By the way, the police were called, and the guards were let go, but only after we had already left the premises, thanks to you. We owe you our gratitude. But before we go off about that stuff ... are you ready for your next assignment?"

" And what might that be?" Jamie asks curiously.

" Theft."

" Ah."

Jamie raises his eyebrows.

" There is a billionaire up in the hills, Jamie. He stole what was rightfully ours. He signed the contract, he broke the deal, and now he will not return our property. We cannot let him get away with this. We are going to break in and retrieve our things. Are you in or not?"

" Of course. What's in it for me?"

" Ha-ha! I like you, Jamie. A share of the cash we steal will be yours. How does 10% sound?"

" Give me 20% and I'll do it," Jamie says.

" Deal. Meet me here at 2:00 p.m. No some other time. That's when this rich guy leaves the house. Well, a little bit before that actually, but it provides us just enough time to take what is actually ours."

Jamie waits till Alexander is out of the room and looks at Devon.

" So, Devon, do you know who gives us the projects?"

" Well, Alexander does, of course," he answers.

" No, no. I mean: Who is above Alexander? Who gives him the projects?"

" Oh, his name is Jake Forsyth, but we don't talk about him. Nobody can even see him. I never have. He manages the entire underground world, that's why. He doesn't trust a lot of people, so it's difficult to get close to him."

" I see," Jamie says.

That afternoon, the trio meets at the same workplace. They put on hoodies to hide their identity, just in case somebody sees them. From there they head to the hills and get in a costly community full of villas and big estates. Jamie has never entered this neighborhood and marvels at the gorgeous yards, the water fountains, fancy statues, and the houses that cost millions.

They pull up on one side of the street, after which Alexander orders them to walk across the street.

" Never park your car on the same side of the street of the house you're going to break in," he teaches.

The house looks huge. Pillars, golden accessories, and sophisticated shapes in the hedges make this home a little paradise for anyone who can afford it. A big swimming pool becomes noticeable as they walk around the back and try to open the back entrance.

Alexander appears to have it easy with all his tricks to break in. Some tools from his backpack, a little drill, and a mirror are sufficient for them to simply open the back entrance without the alarm going off.

" Spread out," Alexander says. "See this? This is what we're trying to find."

He shows a photograph of a diamond helmet. It looks glossy and expensive. No doubt this item costs millions.

" And this," Alexander adds.

Another photo portrays a golden axe.

" Is that pure gold?" Jamie asks.

" Yes, so now you comprehend why it deserves so much. But keep your voice down, please. We are presuming there is no one in the house, but you can never make certain."

The three of them broke up. Jamie goes upstairs, Devon comes down to the basement, and Alexander remains on the primary floor. Each of them browses the house thoroughly. Jamie finds the axe in a drawer hidden in a walk-in closet. Devon finds the diamond helmet in a chest somewhere deep in the basement. Both of them meet on the main floor.

" Good," Alexander says. "And do you know what, guys ... I found a few thousand bucks in the closet. This guy is loaded. Money is just coming out of the cracks in this home. Anyway, let's get out of here. We are done. We got what we needed, so let's not stay here for another minute."

They leave the house and gently close the door, giving the owner the impression that absolutely nothing has been changed.

" Watch out, the owner is back," Alexander says.

Jamie and Alexander dive into the bushes, but Devon trips over his own feet and falls down into the swimming pool.

SPLASH!

The owner discovered us. It's clear. He looks up as if he heard the sound originating from the pool. He walks to his home but takes a detour to discover what is going on in the swimming pool. Devon remains under water.

" We've got to help him," Jamie says.

" There's nothing we can do," Alexander says. "It would be better to leave. His fate is regrettable, but we've got to go or we'll all be in trouble."

" No, we can't just leave him," Jamie argues.

" Then get him if you want. I have the helmet and the axe. There is no point in helping him."

" Just give me two minutes," Jamie insists.

" Okay, but no longer," Alexander says. "We have to leave as fast as we can. If you're not back within 2 minutes, I will leave without you."

" That's not gonna happen," Jamie says.

He examines if the coast is clear. It isn't. The millionaire is standing close to the water now, suspicious that somebody has trespassed and is hiding someplace not too far away from him. He is looking to the right and to the left. Then he looks down at the swimming pool.

" Hey!" he says.

At that moment Jamie dashes at him and pushes him into the pool.

" Come on," he says to Devon as he extends his hand.

Devon grabs his hand and Jamie pulls up the deserted bad guy. Together they run as fast as they can, reaching the car before the rich owner of the house even realizes who that was and what just happened to him. The duo enters into the car and tells Alexander to drive. As quickly as they can they drive away, happy with the two valuable objects they just took.

" Thanks for getting me," Devon says. "I do not know what would have happened if he would have found me first."

" You're welcome," Jamie says.

" You're a funny guy, Jamie," Alexander says. "You are a tough negotiator, you don't care about breaking the law, but you do everything to secure the life of another crimi ... uhm ... coworker."

Jamie smiles. He didn't do this without some reason. It's not that he cares if a dumb bad guy like Devon gets arrested, but he has other intentions ... intentions they will quickly all learn about.

" We have another task for you," Alexander says as they get to the workplace.
" I 'd like to see my 20% first," Jamie says.
" Oh yeah, ha-ha! I almost forgot. I truly did."
" Right," Jamie says skeptically.
Alexander pays Jamie.
" That's 20% of what these objects are worth if we sold them. We will deal with it, but this is just a payment in advance, also to keep you on your feet for the next task."
" Go ahead," Jamie says.
" It's easy," Alexander says. "Have you heard of multi-level marketing companies?"
" Remind me," Jamie says.
" Multi-level marketing companies let you in if you give them an amount of money and promise that you can make a lot more if you sell their item. Let's say that their product is oils ... you know ... those oils you can smell or put in your drink for health. A business would request $100 of your money and tell you that you can make $100,000 in a year back if you sell their oils to clients, like friends, family, and associates. If they register underneath you, you get a portion if they sell something. By doing this, if you get to the top, you'll have all those people working under you and you can earn money without doing anything. Get it?"
" Sure. Sounds familiar. But are you actually trying to tell me that you have a company like that?" Jamie asks.
" Similar. What we have is called a pyramid scam. It's the same concept, but there is no real product to sell, so they will think they can make their money back, but before they know it, it's already too late and you'll be out the door with their money. All you have to do, is convince people how much they can make back if they only invest a little."
" I can do that. Where can I find these people?"
" We already prepared a list of potential customers who have shown at least some interest," Alexander replies. "It is probably easy. Go to their doors, talk to them, and for every individual who registers, you get 50%."
" Give me that list, and I'll show you how it's done," Jamie says.
" That's the spirit! You have a week to complete this list. Strive for the top, and you'll be a lot wealthier by the end of the week. Any questions?"
" Not really. All the information is on there, isn't it?"
" Exactly. Now go get them."
The first door. It took a while to get there, and Jamie hasn't knocked on doors since a few years ago when he was selling knives and had an even harder time making ends meet. He walks through the small gate and knocks. It takes a minute before the resident opens. It's an old man with glasses and a dark blue t-shirt. His belt looks way too high and his expression is really naïve to say the least.
" Hi there, boy. What can I do for you?"
" How would you like to make a $1000 residual income?" Jamie asks.
" Well, uhm ..."
" Let me just introduce myself. My name is Jack. I have been in this business for only a few years now and I am already making 6 figures."
" You are telling me that you already make $100,000 each year?" the old man asks.

" Hey, don't take my word for it. Just enroll in the program. We have numerous people who are making a comparable amount of money each year and have hardly begun. All you need to do, is invest $100, which you can make back within a few weeks. Once you're past that point, it's all profit and you can purchase that beautiful home you always imagined, go on a trip to a tropical paradise, or contribute some money to a charity provide education for those in need. Just think of the possibilities!"

Jamie says a lot more to convince the old man and gathers his $100. After another door, and another, and another ... he is surpassing his own expectations. This is too easy! All these people are quickly succumbing to this dumb scam. All he has to do, is keep up the smooth talking and put a few persuading factors out there and they sign up, handing him their money.

For an entire week, he works as hard as he can. He visits people in the morning, the afternoon, and even in the evening. He knocks on door after door, often sprinting to the next door to get it done much faster. Some people do not want to hear it and don't fall for his tricking words. They have already been conned out of their money a lot of times. But the majority of the people on the list are open and going to invest a little, gullible as children, believing that they will get wealthy by investing into this pyramid scheme.

Chapter 6: Cops All over the Place

The last day of the week, and coincidentally the last door Jamie knocks on, a police officer pulls over. He has been following Jamie for a few hours now, attempting to pick up some of the things Jamie says to the potential clients on the list. He does not trust it one bit.

Jamie returns after speaking to the woman at the door. He avoids the small barking pet dog that appears more courageous than its size.

" Hold on, there. I'm Officer Sykes. Can I please see your business license?"

" Yeah, I got it right here," Jamie says as he looks into his bag for paperwork.

He doesn't actually have a business license, but he is pretending to get it. A few seconds afterwards, he takes a paper and throws it at the police officer. The officer tries to catch it, startled by the abrupt action of this guy. He grabs the piece of paper on the ground and looks up, knowing that he has been deceived. Jamie is already a hundred feet away, taking the opportunity to escape.

" Come back here!" Officer Sykes yells.

He gets his walkie-talkie.

" Request for instant backup. Suspect is running away on Third Street and 21st Avenue."

He steps into his car, puts on his siren, and chases after Jamie. Wait a minute. Where did he go? He must have gone into that street. Other police cars are approaching, but they have totally lost sight of him.

" What the ...? He can't be too far. Scan the area completely!" Officer Sykes commands. But it's no use. Jamie has already jumped into a sewage system and is patient enough to wait there for days if he needs to. It stinks, and he is a little annoyed that he got caught, but he got away and that's what counts. Night falls, and the officers are slowly being called off duty. They've quit. They think he left. Jamie is waiting for another hour after he sees all the police vehicles leave, and then climbs out of the sewer. He goes to Counter's office and reports.

" Oh my, you stink, man," Alexander grumbles.

" I got into trouble. There were some police officers following me."

" Wow, and you dove into the sewer? I got ta tell ya, you got commitment, man."

" Thanks. Here is the cash I earned."

Alexander counts it and gives Jamie half of it.

" I'm amazed," he says. "In fact, I've been speaking to my supervisor and he is willing to see you. He's heard of your accomplishments and wishes to meet you face to face."

Jamie tries to manage his enthusiasm.

" Ah, good," he says calmly, though exuberantly jumping up and down inside.

" You'll meet him tomorrow," Alexander says. "Now go home and enjoy your money." Jamie walks home past the familiar streets in his neighborhood. He understands what he's done. He has scammed hundreds of people out of their money. He's not happy with it, but he has a mission. When he gets back, he counts his money again and is grateful that he can pay the rental money ahead of time, just so he doesn't need to stress over it for a few months. He kicks back and practices meditation for some time, relaxing and getting ready for the big day that he can meet Jake Forsyth.

" It's about time," he thinks. "A criminal mastermind like him needs to show their face every once in a while."

Chapter 7: The Big Boss

Jamie is on time. He is sure of that. He doesn't want to miss this appointment. He is blindfolded. Alexander and Devon ensured that Jamie would know absolutely nothing about the place of the big boss, Jake Forsyth.

Jamie doesn't care. All he wants, is to meet the man. He has been anticipating it for a while now and understands that he has gotten to a level that one who is in charge finally started trusting him.

The car arrives. Jamie is pushed out of the car. Devon removes the blindfold. Jamie looks around. They are inside a garage of some storage facility. He doesn't recognize it, but it does not matter. He just needs to know where Jake Forsyth is. Devon pushes him towards a door.

" Take it easy," Jamie says.

" Hey, just because you got me out of trouble once, does not mean you can have a big mouth," Devon says. "So shut up and keep walking."

" Thanks for nothing... pffft....," Jamie grumbles silently.

They walk through a luxurious hallway, with red carpet on the floor, expensive mirrors on the walls, and realistic paintings on each side. The chandeliers must have cost a fortune, Jamie figures.

A little later, they arrive at a wooden door, carved with patterns and lavish paintings of lions, tigers, and other fierce animals. They knock. For a moment, it's silent on the other end.

" Come in," they all of a sudden hear.

Jamie is pushed inside and stands face to face with Counter's prominent leader. Jake Forsyth is a huge guy in a suit, with the same costly sunglasses as Jamie is wearing. He has a red tie and leather shoes. With a big-headed little twirl in his step, he approaches Jamie and observes him, walking around him and attempting to be intimidating.

" So," he starts. "You must be Jamie. I heard a lot about you. Do you know why I called you here?"

" You wanted to praise me for my efficiency, sir?" Jamie asks while pushing a small, secret button on the back of his suit.

" That too," Jake Forsyth says. "I have to admit I am pleased. You exchanged crucial tax documents, took out 10 guards at the docks, helped smuggle fa ... uhm ... some real money into the nation, you obtained stolen objects from a corrupt minister, flew to the rescue when one of our colleagues was stuck, and spent an entire week registering more people for our pyramid sc ... uhm ... multilevel marketing business than anyone else has."

" For Counter I'd do anything, sir," Jamie says.

" Yes, I saw that, which brings me to the following: Our data say that you registered 246 people this week. Is that correct?"

" Uhm ... I-I believe so," Jamie stutters.

Jake Forsyth comes closer and gets a little in Jamie's face.

" You little snake, did you think I was an idiot? That I wouldn't discover what you're trying to do?" he unexpectedly asks.

" I do not know what you're referring to," Jamie says.

" Let me clarify. I had math in school like any other kid," Jake Forsyth says. "If you truly registered 245 people, you should have earned $24,600. Correct?"
" I guess so. I didn't count," Jamie says.
" Well, Alexander swears he provided you half of that money, which is 50%. That must be an amount of $12,300. That leaves me the same amount."
" Okay, sir. I do not see the problem here."
" I got $20,300 back!" he all of a sudden yells loudly in anger. "Would you care to tell me where the $8,000 came from?! Certainly, it wasn't a contribution from Alexander! What is going on here ?!"
" Oh that?" Jamie asks. "Why do you care? Now you have more money, so what are you complaining about?"
" Don't talk back to me, boy," he says degradingly. "I know you're up to something. You must have included that amount of money in there. At first, I was astonished at the amount you made, which is why I requested for your arrival. I wanted to see you because I was impressed and wanted to thank you. But then, when I counted the subscribers and the money again, I knew something was wrong. You put your own money with it to give me a reward or something. Why?"
" Oh, well ... you see ..."
But before Jamie can say another word, the police kick in the door.
Bam!
" Put your hands above your head and kneel on the floor now!" one of the cops says.
Jake Forsyth obediently kneels down and looks at Jamie. But Jamie isn't kneeling down. He smiles and shakes the cop's hand. Then he walks to Jake Forsyth and bends over in front of him, looking him directly in the eyes.
" I guess I don't need to really explain myself any longer, do I?" he says smilingly. "The only reason I committed all those criminal activities was to earn your trust. Including my own money was just a good way to impress you, so that you would talk to me and show me where you were hiding. It was difficult to find out where you were, and the police were dying to know where to go to get you. They've looked all over the city, and the best way to get near you and discover your location was to have an insider."
" But you took so much! Do not you feel guilty?" Jake Forsyth asks.
" Not truly. The police have all my money. They have the addresses and they know precisely whom to give it back to. No one lost their money forever, just temporarily."
" How could you ?! I gave you everything. I trusted you. You could have been a wealthy man. Why would you give that up?"
" I 'd rather be honest," Jamie answers. "Besides, the police are paying me well for this little espionage. They interviewed me elaborately to know if I was the right guy, and I think that I have proved that I am."
Jamie winks at the officer next to him.
" Yes, you have," the officer says. "By the way, sorry about the chase and your little adventure in the sewage system. Those men didn't know about our little deal, so they just chased you without realizing you were on a mission."

" It's all right," Jamie says. "Thanks to my new income, I purchased a new showerhead. Men, take this criminal away!"

" Hey, I'm supposed to say that," the officer says.

" Sorry, I just always wanted to do that," Jamie says as he shrugs.

" Just you wait! I'll get you! I'll find you and it won't matter where you will be hiding!" Jake Forsyth shouts as he is being dragged over the floor towards the outside door.

" Yeah, yeah, sure," Jamie says with a smile.

THE END

Love Potion Number 1

Chapter 1: Recipes

I was almost there; the perfect potion was within my reach. What is the perfect potion? Well, the one that grants you eternal youth, of course. I knew it existed. I had heard of it often times before, but it was as if it was some secret recipe handed down throughout generations. I am sure a ton of witches had already used it and were now experiencing the terrific effects of living forever. But I wasn't ...

I got up that day. It was a bright morning, and I have to confess I was a little inflamed because the light had woken me up. I yawned, I extended my arms and legs, and in my underclothing, I walked to the restroom. I was looking in the mirror.

" Holy guacamole!" I exclaimed.

I had just discovered the dreadful state my hair was in. It was a giantl mess. And despite the fact that I wouldn't head out to meet anybody today, I always considered looking after myself a big concern.

Oh, did I tell you my name? I actually forgot. Let me introduce myself. I am Sasha and I am 25 years old. My mother and father love me, but they were a little really strict. Yeah, it was pretty bad.

They were so uptight that they made sure I was always on time; I always had to look like a doll; I always had to watch my manners at the table; I always had to get good results in school; I always needed to ... fine, you understand, don't you? They were perfectionists. But not me. Because although I am looking for the perfect potion, I really do not care about perfectionism. Not everything needs to be exactly right. You can be a little off and still manage to do great, do not you think?

That's how it was with me. I was always a little off. I dropped off to sleep throughout witch classes. Oh, did I mention my mother is a witch? Well, there you go; I said it. She is. And she wanted my career as a witch as well. She constantly told me about the benefits of magic, real magic, as she used to say. My dad concurred, of course, so I was sent out to various schools in the district that taught the art of witchcraft. And when I say "witchcraft," I am obviously describing the white kind.

No, I do not do that evil, dark stuff. "Black magic" is simply not an alternative for me. Anyway, so I was saying something about being "off." Here is the important things: I was dyslexic, which means I have a tough time reading. I thought the letter "p" and the letter "q" looked the same, and I could never understand the distinction between the letters "d" and "b" if you know what I mean. It's a miracle my journal isn't filled with spealling mystakes, or is it? Oh, who cares, as long as you can read it, right?

Another thing that was a little "off" about me, was my inability of concentration. The world is beautiful. I was so happy to see colors, hear noises and music, and perceive all the different smells around me. It was hard for me to block everything else out and focus on one job. It was like an overload of the senses.

With these quirks, I wasn't that good for school. I moved from one school to the other, only to find myself in another class with all kinds of girls who were supposed to be the smartest ones in town but didn't even know how to look great.

I knew how to look great.

A lot of people were interested in me. They always looked when I walked by, and a few of would always whistle. When there was a dance, each guy would stand in line to take me there. I could choose easily between them, and the other ladies watched in awe, extremely envious of the flirty habits that just came naturally to me.

So yes, I was a real looker, but I just didn't feel wise. I felt like I was dumb. I felt as if I belonged at a school with a lot of fashion models, but not witches. Witchcraft (again, the good kind) was difficult! Each time I tried to put the elements together that I thought were described in the old, dirty books, I wound up making some silly mistake, which triggered the whole brew to boil over or would become the wrong color.

But it was over now. I had quit on school. I was going to do it mySELF! When I told my parents, my mother encouraged me and wished me luck, but my father was as stern as ever.

" You better return with something worthwhile," he said when I left.

I assured him that I would, but I had no clue how it was going to work. I left town and went to reside in a peaceful hideout on the other side of the mountains. It was a cozy cottage, so I didn't mind, but I was awfully lonesome in some cases.

Nevertheless, I was determined to show the best formula and the best potion to my parents. They would be proud of me ... they'd be incredibly happy! Yep. That was my motivation: To show my parents. I think we all have that a bit; that our whole purpose in life is to get our parents' attention.

So here I was in my home, collecting the toe of a rat, a cow's hair, and a few magic mushrooms. The cauldron was huge. The smells from it weren't very good any longer, but I was following the directions in the huge magic book and was stirring heavily to get these fluids going.

When I looked for the lemon pepper, I bumped my head.
" Ouch!" I said.
Then I heard another sound, "Meow!"
" Hey, Whiskas. What are you doing here? I thought you were searching for mice."
" Meow," was the answer.
If only I had created a potion to speak "cat." That would have been valuable. Now Whiskas was purring. He was annoying me a little.
" Okay, that's enough," I said. "You can go do something else now."
The cat kept rubbing its side against my leg. I wasn't too pleased with it, and I felt like kicking it away.
" That's enough!" I yelled. "I am busy! Sorry, Whiskas. Some other time will be better."
But Whiskas would not go away. Instead, he ended up being fussy and began meowing louder and louder. He ran around in circles and would not leave the room even after I opened the door.
" Go already!" I said.
Clumsy cat! It walked backwards and knocked me over, so that I fell and ran into the cauldron. The fluids in the cauldron streamed over and dropped into my t-shirt.
" Ouch!" I said again. "This is it! You are leaving. NOW!"
I took the cat and held it in front of me. I immediately walked to the door, said, "Cat-a-pult!" and tossed him out the door. Did you know cats do not always land on their paws? Poor Whiskas landed on his face. I felt a little bad afterwards.
Thud!
I was just grateful it didn't actually burn my skin.
I chose to look at the damage. I got a rag and cleaned up the remainder of the mess. Luckily, it wasn't really bad.
I continued with the formula, the descriptions and the complex chemical explanations in the book I was using. The book was of ancient origins. It was made a few thousand years ago and handed down to me. Witchcraft isn't simple. You can't just create a magical item or potion. It all needs to be done according to specific steps, and the specific extract of each additive is required to make it work. To put it simply, it was quite difficult.

Take 2 teaspoons of vinegar, blend it with a snake's tail, an end of 11 inches, put a raindrop from the high mountains in it, stir often, and then sprinkle 3 particles from the explosive impacts of a big explosion before including a skeleton's eye.

And that's just one of the 20 paragraphs I had to read for one recipe. But this was the supreme recipe! And fortunately, I had the majority of these ingredients anyway. You may wonder where you can find a skeleton's eye or the particles from a big explosion, but I have to admit that I was impressed with the schools' supplies and just how much they wanted to sell to me at a low price. All I had to do, was integrate them.
" Okay, a little bit of this ... and then this ... it's coming. I think I am nearly done."
I added the last active ingredients.
BOOOOOM!!!!

The fluids exploded and splashed all over my room. The entire floor was disgusting; it was everywhere. I was dissatisfied and covered in a hot type of soup. Yuck! But more than anything I just wanted to find out what had gone wrong.

I scanned the book again, going over all the steps I followed. Pearls ... check ... fish bone ... check ... 20 grains of salt ... check ... oh such perfectionism! But what was that? Only 2 teaspoons of vinegar? Oh no! I put 5 in! It's that dumb dyslexia I am fighting with. Why did the one who created the alphabet or numbers or something make the 2 and the 5 appear so similar? Ughh ... now my potion was messed up and I had to do it all over again.

Another day, another mistake. Back to the start ... it was all part of my routine. But someday, I would master this thing.

Chapter 3: The Equivalent of It

I didn't know what was going to happen to me ... till that dark day arrived. It was my nemesis, a woman from one of the witch schools who was bitter and upset. Her name was Naomi. She was always unpleasant, and she wasn't very friendly. I still remembered that whenever I had class with her, back then that I still went to school, she would take me apart and humiliate me in front of the whole class.

One time, for example, she made me bend all the way over and touch my toes. I had no idea why, but I obeyed blindly. Later on, I knew that she just wanted me to screw up my hair I had so thoroughly done that early morning, but instead of everybody laughing at me, I got some attention from guys who were looking closely, and were somewhat hypnotized by my beautiful body. I do not think I want to speak about that a lot, but all I can say, is that a few of them came to me after class and asked me on dates. Maybe they had seen my underwear under my skirt. It only gave me more attention, and I saw Naomi, my instructor, become green with jealousy.

She disliked me. Why? Because I was attractive and she wasn't. Her face wasn't really symmetrical, she had an enormous nose, and her black hat didn't go along with her attire ... I could tell, particularly with my sense of fashion.

So one day, I was just minding my own business in my tiny home, fiddling with the components I had and re-reading the formula in my book, when I heard a knock on the door.

I opened the door.

" Whaahaa! Yeehee!" she said.

There she was, not even waiting for me to talk to me. She knocked me over and I fell on the floor. It appeared to take place a lot lately. First by the cat, and then by ... oh well, anyway, she ran towards my books, nabbed the ancient book with the formula from the table, and exclaimed evil witch sounds.

I always knew there was something fishy about her. But when she said that she wanted the formula for fountain of youth to reverse it and make everyone ugly, so that she would not be considered as such, I truly knew she was messed up.

In one way, I felt for her, but the other half of my conscience told me to intervene.

" Give it back!" I yelled.

" No way, you irritating 'model,'" she said sarcastically. "I am going to do the opposite of what's in this book, and when I have figured it out, you will be the first one to turn ugly."

" What did I ever do to you? Are you truly that bitter that you want to turn everybody ugly?"

No response. She stepped on her broomstick and flew away. I ran back inside and got mine. The chase had started.

That evil witch. How dare she steal my recipe book? How dare she design such wicked schemes? I was focused and upset. I was going to stop her forever.

When I grabbed my broomstick, I saw Whiskas standing in the corner. He looked at me with pitiful eyes, as if he was excusing the previous accident he had caused. Poor cat. Maybe I could take him with me. He could come in handy.

Oh, what was I saying? He would just be in the way, just like before.

But then I checked out those big, cute eyes and I could not resist him. I decided to pick him up and put him at the back of my broomstick.

" You better behave," I told him.

Then I took off.

Flying through the air is a ton of fun. It's one of the terrific benefits of being a witch. I have always loved it. And this time, I had to go much faster than ever, because I was chasing my mortal enemy, the bothersome Naomi with all her self-confidence concerns, the one who took out all her problems on me, although I never did anything on purpose to make her feel bad. It was absurd, and it just wasn't fair.

I saw her. She had become a little dot in the distance, and I do not know if she saw me following her, but one thing was for sure: I knew where I was going. It took about 20 minutes till I saw her descend and land someplace in the woods. I decided to keep my distance, so I landed elsewhere. From afar, I spied on her. I discovered that she had a little cottage herself, but hers was deep in the forest, not just visible for everyone to see, like mine. It felt more like a secret agent or something this way, and I wondered what she was hiding in there.

I snuck closer. She had already gone inside.

" Meow," Whiskas said.

" Ssshh ..." I said, holding my finger in front of my mouth and looking at him.

I was talking to a cat. I felt a little silly.

Together, we came to the cottage but we still hid outside. I looked through the window and saw Naomi staring at the book. I didn't know yet how I was going to get the book back, but I knew I would come up with something. I always did.

I looked at Whiskas. Then I looked through the window.

I looked at Whiskas again. I looked through the window again.

Ha! I knew what to do. I just needed a distraction. Whiskas didn't look pleased when I squinted my eyes and had a smirk on my face. He slowly began leaving, but I was much faster.

" I am sorry, Whiskas," I said. "It's nothing personal at all."

I pulled back my leg and threw the cat as far as I could.

" Meowowowow!" the cat said.

He flew through the air and ended on his paws this time. Fortunately, this caught Naomi's attention. She looked over and came through the door. When she came outside and looked the other way, I quickly snuck around the back and went through the back door to take my book back. She was still looking around, wondering where the crying cat sound came from.

Good.

This was good.

I had the book. I was going to take it home, and she would never know how it disappeared, or would she?

Chapter 5: Awkward Witch

I tripped! When I was going out the back door, I tripped and fell, taking pots and pans down with me.

Cling! Clang! Clingeling!

The noise was deafening. Oh no, she would find me!

" Hahah! I've got you now," she said.

She walked over fast and pulled the book out of my hands.

" You will not be in my way anymore," she said.

" Wait, why do you have to be this way?" I asked. "It doesn't make any sense, Naomi. You do not need to hate everybody because you feel bad about yourself."

" Ha! Are you trying to talk me down? That's not going to work. Everybody dislikes my face. They deserve to know how it feels."

" No, they don't," I said.

" Oh, it's so simple for you to say," she said. "You were always popular and wanted. I never had any of that. People think I am ugly."

" But what if we could make your face prettier? Would not that make it better? Then you wouldn't have to bug anyone else. You could just leave them the way they are."

" Apparently you don't know anything about these recipes. The fountain of youth potion only helps you stay young, but it does not improve your face."

" Well, isn't there a potion that can help you become beautiful?" I asked.

" There is," she said calmly. Then she put her head down and became extremely sad. I saw that she had been dealing with this issue for a while now. It was consuming her, and she could not let it go.

It made me think of how much of a priority it is to people, maybe even more to women, to be considered good-looking. When they think they're ugly, even when they are not, it can truly harm their self-esteem. I was hoping I could do something to help, so she wouldn't take out her disappointment on others.

" And?" I asked. "Where is the recipe?"

She sobbed. "It's right there in this book."

" Oh. Then it shouldn't be a problem. Here, let me look it up."

I started skimming the pages of the book, searching for the formula for the beauty potion. I couldn't find it, so I searched in the content page.

" It's on page 288," she said, interrupting me. "I already looked at it."

" Ah, so you are familiar with it. How come you haven't brewed it yet?"

Chapter 6: That Component We Looked for

Naomi looked sad again, as if she had been attempting to do it her entire life and had been quitting at every attempt. She buried her face in her hands. I put my hand on her back on rubbed her back a little. I apologized for not understanding and asked her again why she hadn't made it yet.

" I have every component I need," she said.

" Let's do it then!" I said excitedly.

" Except for one."

" Oh. What is it?"

" It's a red pearl," she said.

" Really? I have pearls in my home. I can just go get them."

" No," she said. "The ones you have are purple. You can find those anywhere."

" A red pearl? I've never heard of that."

" It's because they are so rare. You can only find them in the Distant Lands. And they are protected by dragons."

" Sounds dangerous," I said.

" It is, and that's why no one I know has ever created that beauty potion yet. Besides, most of other witches look prettier than me anyway."

I thought for a while. If I would brew that potion, I wouldn't just help Naomi and make certain she would stop bugging me, but I would also have the opportunity to take it home and show my parents I made one of the most wanted, hardest to create ... potions in the country, perhaps even on the planet!

" I'm in," I said. "I will go and get the red pearl for you."

" Oh no," Naomi said. "I can't ask you to do that."

" You're not asking me. I am offering my services to you. I want this potion as much as you do."

" Why? You already look terrific. You don't need it."

" Oh, I have my reasons. Trust me."

" Okay, just beware out there. I am not coming with you. I feel too old for experiences with dragons and rocky roads."

" It does not matter. But I want you to do me a favor as well."

" Oh, anything," she said. "If you want to get that pearl for me, just ask what you want."

" Could you look after Whiskas? I've been a little mean to him, but I am sure you will find some yummy milk for him to drink."

" That's all? Yes, of course."

" Thanks. I will see you later."

Those were my last words at the time. I walked outside, got on my broomstick and took off, flying though the sky, all set to face some real dangers.

The Distant Lands were grim and empty. When I showed up there, I couldn't believe a place like this existed. The cooling wind wasn't enough to terrify me. Nevertheless, when I saw dead animal carcasses and flies buzzing around them, I started doubting if I made the correct choice to come here.

Was beauty truly worth all of this? Maybe it was harder for me to understand anyway, since I had been gorgeous all my life. I didn't know any better than getting compliments and attention from everybody daily.

I flew and flew. It was a huge area of rocks and canyons, but no life. The occasional tree provided me hope, but when I discovered that even the bushes were as dry as the desert itself, it really gave me the creeps. A black fog emerged from the distance, making the place seem eerie and bleak, removing all my self-induced peace of mind and faked confidence I had been talking myself into having. What an awful place! Not surprising that Naomi was so reluctant to come here.

I knew where the dragons were. It actually wasn't that tough to find them, since they were always spitting fire and smoke, vaporized from the areas they resided in. So all I had to do, was follow the smoke. I gazed at the horizon while hovering above the ground on my broomstick. I guess I should have floated a bit higher, because at that moment, an ocelot jumped at me! I do not know why I didn't see it coming. Perhaps because it was hiding between some blades of high grass before it assaulted me. In any case, it got on my broomstick.

I figured I had become pretty proficient at kicking and throwing cats anyway, so an ocelot was no different.

" Get off, dumb ocelot!" I yelled, attempting to spin my broomstick in such a way that it would let go.

It didn't let go off it, so I flew around. I went upside down, and made circles to the left and to the right. I spun in the air and shook backward and forward.

" Growowow!" the ocelot said.

It held on for a while, but eventually, it had to let go. I was making too many fast maneuvers on my broomstick to lose him. When I went straight up and dashed down again, only to skim the surface and fly back up again, the ocelot could not hold anymore and fell on the ground.

THUD!

Finally.

Now I could continue my journey. Better to stay high in the sky, unless there were dangerous birds that could attack me. Imagine that. Ughh ...

I put my hand above my eyes and scanned the surface, looking for smoke. Aha! There it was. Vaporizing smoke from behind the range of mountains ... that's where I could find the dragons. I didn't wait any longer and headed into that direction.

When I got there, I could not believe my eyes.

There was lava everywhere. Little lights in the sky and gravity-beating objects were floating above the volcanic rims as if nature didn't have anything to say against it. It was breathtaking and dangerous at the same time. Now I really wasn't sure if I wanted to go on, but I did.

I flew over one of the volcanoes and discovered a dragon. It was primarily black, which made it even harder to follow its motions as it flew away. Another chase, another pursue ... I was pursuing it.

I flew as quick as I could on my broomstick. The dragon flew up into the foggy clouds and back down to the surface area. With every move, I copied its precise pattern. I still didn't know where the pearls were, however. I had been searching for them since I came here, but I didn't see a dragon's nest or a cave or anything. The only thing I could think of, was to keep observing the dragon.

So I waited.

Hiding behind a rock, I waited and waited.

Unexpectedly, a big shadow fell over me. It shocked me, and I turned around to see where it was originating from. It was another dragon!

" Aaaah!" I shrieked in fear, moving up into the sky on my broomstick. The dragon chased after me and sped through the air. I zigzagged to get rid of him but ended up in a foggy cloud. It was gone.

Pfew! That was close. Where did it go? Well, hopefully, it wouldn't return. I think I made a smart move hiding in here.

I waited for another 20 minutes or so before I needed the guts to descend to those frightening areas again. When I did, I finally saw it.

There it was: A red pearl.

But it wasn't easy to get it. It was impossible, or so it appeared to be.

Remember those floating pieces of burning things I was talking about? That's where the red pearls were. I flew closer and took a keen look at one of them. The red pearl was precisely in the core of the burning fire. It didn't make any sense to me how this could be, but there was nothing I could do about it.

Now what?

I couldn't take the entire flaming blaze, could I?

Or maybe I could reach inside it, get the red pearl, and pull it out. But then I would burn my hand! I wasn't going to do that! That would be insane!

I flew to a few other ones to check if they were just as hard to get. Every one of those pearls had the same issue. They were all deep inside the core of a hot, burning item. I figured it was because that was the way they came to existence in the first place: They were naturally and gradually created by the fire in those things. Intriguing, but how was I going to get them out? I flew from the one to the other, ensuring there wasn't a simpler one to obtain.

There wasn't.

Then I did something I have sometimes wondered about later. I frequently asked myself in the following years if it was the best solution, or if it was plain stupidity, because looking back, I shiver when I think back about the pain I went through at that moment.

A fast thought entered my mind: If I would reach inside and grab it, I would burn my hand, but I could take it home, develop the potion and heal my hand with it. The potion grants the ultimate beauty, so drinking it would recover my flawed hand immediately. I was skeptical, but taking courage, I decided there was no other way.

I close my eyes, took a deep breath, and opened my eyes again.

This was it.

I was going to voluntarily burn my hand to help Naomi become stunning.

I could not even imagine the pain I was about to face, but it was needed and I was going to bite through it.

I reached as quickly as I could and got the red pearl with my left hand.

" Ouch!" I shrieked in pain, after which I dropped the pearl and began blowing on my hand. "Owowowow!" I continued, crying in the meantime.

I don't think I had ever felt that much pain before. It was terrible. But I had succeeded. The red pearl was now out of the flaming item. It had fallen to the ground and was now cooling off, so I could put it in my pocket and go home.

I waited a bit, periodically checking the heat that was originating from the red pearl. When I saw that it had become colder, I decided to pick it up, took it with me and whooshed as quickly as I could towards the deserted lands I had travelled through.

Oh, my hand hurt soooo much! But I knew that if I could reach the cottage, it would all soon be over.

After an hour or so, I saw the forest. This was my rescue. Now we just had to create the potion.

Chapter 8: Beauty Potion

When I came to Naomi's home in the forest, I jumped off my broomstick and barged in.
" Naomi!" I yelled. "Let's get that potion going. Now!"
Naomi was stunned. She didn't understand why I was in such a rush. But then she saw my hand and put her hand in front of her mouth.
" What happened?" she asked.
" Only that your precious little pearl was in an excruciating burning flame," I said while flapping my left hand up and down.
" Okay, okay," she said as she was stressing out. "Give me a few seconds. The recipe book. Over there. Okay. The ingredients. Where is the ..."
And that's how it went on for a long time. I walked backward and forward, attempting to forget the pain and helping her when she needed me. I handed her the red pearl from my pocket and we included every little component we had to, according to the instructions in the book. Finally, we put some sage and eggplant in and watched as the fluids in the cauldron turned into a red color.
" Well, this is it then, isn't it?" Naomi asked. "This should be right. Let's wish for the best. After you."
She took the big spoon, dipped it in and gave it to me. I didn't wait another second and drank everything. Suddenly, I felt better. I got a tingling feeling in my hand and I saw it heal quickly. Some other little imperfections in my look altered, but I mostly stayed the same. One thing I noticed but that I didn't tell Naomi, was that all hair on my body disappeared, with the exception for on my head. It was good ... all hair ... arms, legs, underarms, and other body parts I will not point out. I think my breasts ended up being a little larger too, and my waist shrunk. It was actually almost too perfect.
" Oh, that feels soooo great!" I said, being happy that it was working.
Naomi was smiling. She was hopeful. I had never seen her this thrilled before. I gave her the spoon and she took a huge sip herself. I watched as her countenance changed into that of a pretty young woman. She wiggled her fingers and toes and picked up a mirror.
" Wow! Is that me?" she asked. She was happy as a clam. "I am stunning and sexy! This is incredible!"
" I agree, just look at you!" I said.
She kept looking at herself in the mirror for a while. Then she turned to me and gave me a hug.
" I am sorry for all the tough times I put you through," she said. "I was just jealous, and I realize now that I was wrong. You went so far to help me out and you even got your hand burned to get the red pearl. Thank you for all you've done."
" Oh, it's all right," I said. "You're welcome."
I was pretty proud of myself. I had actually helped somebody feel better about herself. It was like a magic makeover. We were like friends all of a sudden. We talked a little before I went home, and I made certain I got a few of the potion's liquids in a giant, glass bottle to take with me. She handed me back the book and I put Whiskas the cat on my broomstick. We flew to my cottage and I went to bed.

The next day, I took a trip to my parents. They had a big home. Whiskas was left at the home. He would just be a drag to take with me. I landed in front of their lawn and walked to the door. I knocked and my mom opened it.

" Welcome!" she said. "You look great!"

Apparently, she had not been expecting me, and she even observed the minor changes in my appearance.

We then gave each other a hug and she let me in. My dad was standing in the hallway. He looked at me with a serious expression on his face. I looked back. It was a little uncomfortable.

" So what did you make?" he asked.

" I made a beauty potion," I said proudly.

I pulled the bottle out of my bag and showed it to them. My mom had already become fairly old, and the wrinkles on her face were definitely showing. So when I said I had a "beauty potion," she seemed really interested.

" I'd like to try it," she said.

My dad looked fascinated too. He came closer and took a long, hard look at the potion, as if he could tell how efficient it would be just by looking at it. My mom opened it up and just took a little sip.

My father took a step back. "Whoa," he said. "What is happening?"

My mother's wrinkles disappeared instantly; her whole appearance ended up being more youthful and smooth. As she felt the rush from the impact of the fluids, a smile appeared on her face.

" It feels excellent," she said.

" Wow, honey," my dad said. "You are ... I can't even find the words for it."

" Pretty good, isn't it?" I said.

" Sasha, my daughter. This is the most excellent thing you've ever made. I am really proud of you."

" Thanks, dad."

" Now if you'll excuse us, I think I want to give my wife a kiss or two."

" Uhm ..."

I didn't know what to do, but before I knew it, they were kissing each other elaborately. My father was starting to take off my mom's t shirt, and that made me feel awkward."

Okay, have fun. I am outta here," I said as I hurried upstairs.

It was a fantastic day. My parents were proud of me. They were happy with each other, and EVEN my dad was proud of me.

And me? I was attempting to figure out my new bra size.

THE END

Interrogating

Investigations

My name is investigator Cory. I am the primary detective in this town. You see, everybody here has heard of me, and I generally know everyone else, but there are many things occurring behind the screens, and I am the one to expose them.
I have always loved puzzles. A puzzle means there is a question. The answer can be found by lining up clues and drawing the correct conclusion. Unsolved puzzles are secrets. They are those things nobody understands just because they do not have the needed knowledge.
I am all about finding the knowledge, and I have the means to determine what happened ... what REALLY happened. Whenever I talk to people, they always have their own version of what occurred. I kind of like being a human lie detector. I watch people's eyes, their posture, their body movement, and I add up the details of their stories and conclude what sounds most plausible. And after that it's up to me to go after some real proof.
Anyway, I just wanted to make clear what I do. I am watchful, I am all about the facts, not fiction. I have a strong desire to find the truth, and that means I must do crazy things sometimes.
I am 29 years old, so some people consider me a novice, but I have studied how to be a detective for many years now, and I know what I am doing. I am single, and sooner or later I will meet the right woman I am sure, but for now, I just focus on work. I love it, it loves me. It's a good bond. Ha! Just listen to me ... talking as if my job is an actual person.
I welcome you to my life. There is always something going on. It's an exhilarating experience.

Murdered

It was pretty nasty when we found her. And with that, I mean more nasty than pretty. The town police was all over it. They saw her dead body on the floor. There was blood and stuff, but I won't bother you with the gruesome details of the scene. Let's just say that she was dead and that it was apparent that someone had stabbed her. The blade was gone, naturally, so it appeared to be a wise enough lawbreaker who found out that hiding the weapon would leave him or her undiscovered.

" Looks like murder. What do you think?" the policeman asked.

His name was Reeves, and he had been solving cases with me for several years now. The majority of them were theft, robbery, or some complicated paperwork confusion, but a murder in this small village was practically unheard of, so both of us were frightened.

" I do not know," I answered. "But it definitely seems to be a stabbing. Perhaps with a dagger, seeing the size and depth of the injury."

" Well, I am going to look around in the remainder of the house," he said. "We may find some other things that can help us find evidence."

" Good idea. Just let me know if you see anything suspicious."

" Will do."

I bent over and observed the rest of the body. She was resting on her side, stabbed in the chest, just once. But I knew these kinds of things weren't always that simple. If I could find other marks, scratches, or injuries, it could indicate a battle, some stuff or dust, or something else that would give me another clue about the killer.

" So tell me more about the victim," I said to one of the police officers.

" Well, her name is Vicky, but you already knew that, didn't you?"

" Yes, I know many people by name here, but what I want, is details. I wish to know about her life: The people she was seeing, her partner, her routine ... everything."

I looked around a little bit longer in the house and found some scratches on the walls. Some blood, but not much. It didn't appear like the victim had had been fighting back for a very long time. I also saw a fluffy feather. Odd. Where did the feather here originate from? I decided to pick it up, I looked at it, and I put it in my pocket.

" I could not find anything," Reeves said as he came downstairs. "You?"

" Just a few items," I said. "But I do not think we'll see any other real clues in here. I am all set to begin questioning some of the villagers. How about you?"

" We ought to begin with the spouse he suggested.

" I completely agree with you. He must know more about the victim than anyone else. After all, it is his own wife. And if he hasn't done it, he could point a few fingers."

" True. But we cannot presume he hasn't done it. There have been plenty reports from other towns of abusive husbands who killed their partners for some reason."

" You are definitely right, Reeves. until we find hard evidence that he is innocent, he is still a suspect."

Suspect 1: Brox

It was afternoon. Vicky's husband was working in his workshop. He was a blacksmith and had a fine reputation as a qualified blacksmith. We both went, Reeves and I; and we found the husband banging his hammer on a piece of metal.
" Good day, Brox," I said.
" Good day, gentlemen," he replied. "What can I help you with?"
" We are here to collect information about your deceased wife."
" Murdered," he corrected us.
" I'm sorry?"
" My murdered wife," he said bitterly. "She didn't just die by accident. Did you actually see the body?"
" Uhm ... yes we did. And you are right. We suspect it was a stabbing."
" And if I get my hands on whoever did it, he is going to pay," he said, after which he started banging his hammer on the steel again. I could see his anger, but I could not discount him from being a suspect yet. I needed a motive, an alibi, a reason for innocence.
BANG! BANG! BANG!
" Excuse me," I said. "Could we please have a word with you?"
He looked at me and said, "I have absolutely nothing to say. I didn't do it."
" Yes, that might hold true, but by asking you some basic questions, we could dig deeper into the matter and maybe find out who did."
In the beginning, he hesitated to cooperate, but then he put his hammer down and welcomed us to sit on a chair behind him. I saw, when we went inside, that it was a beautiful workshop. The steel was adequately organized, and the results of his effort were hanging on the walls. If anybody would have a murder weapon, it would be this man. The knives, swords, and axes he created were sharp and strong, and my eye saw a knife with blood on it. Nevertheless, I wasn't going to point it out instantly, as I didn't want him to think as if I was condemning him of anything, so I decided to hold my tongue for now.
" Tell us about the night of the murder," Reeves said.
" Well," Brox began. "I was out in the bar with my friends. You know, I just do that every weekend to have some fun. I was there later than normal, and I have to confess that I didn't get home until 5 in the morning the next day. A lot of times, it's not like that, though."
" Go on," I said.
" And then she was there. I thought she had just passed out, but when I tried to wake her up, I saw the blood and found that she was dead."
" What time was it when you found your partner?"
" It was a little after 5 in the morning, like I said."
" Your story makes sense, Brox, except for the fact that you got the police at 9, so 4 hours later. How come you didn't get the police immediately? Seeing your spouse dead on the floor sounds like an emergency to me. Didn't you think it was important enough to inform us?"
" Oh, well, the thing about that is ... uhm ... I couldn't find the police headquarters."
" You could not find the police headquarters? How many years have you lived here?"

" Come on, guys, it was dark and you know how all these streets look the same."
" Still, Brox, it only takes 15 minutes to arrive. Would you mind explaining us why it took you 4 hours?"
He was silent. It was obvious that he was hiding something. His hands began fidgeting and he didn't look me in the eyes any longer. I didn't know if that made him more of a suspect than anyone else or if something even worse was going on.
" Brox," I said again.
" Fine," he said in an agitated voice. "I fell asleep, okay? I just drank too much and when I saw my spouse, I lost my balance and crashed out on the bed. Are you happy now? I am sorry that I didn't get anybody, but that's just what happened."
" I do not like your drinking habits, but understanding that you went to sleep makes you less of a suspect, so it's crucial that we understand these things."
" I didn't do it! Are you getting that in your fat skull? Am I making any sense? Why would I kill my own wife?"
" That's a good question," I said. "Can you tell me more about your relationship with her?"
" Oh, now you would like to know about my marital relationship. Well, let me tell you ... it's none of your business."
" There is a murderer in the area," I answered. "So yes, it is our business. If you don't comply, we have permission to arrest you. So please answer the question."
He became much more annoyed. Poor guy. He banged his fist on the table and blurted it out.
" It was bad! It was truly bad! We have been married for 15 years now and something happened. I do not even know what I did wrong, but each time I went to the bar in the weekend, I found her with some other man in our house."
" Do you think she was cheating on you?"
" Yes, I presume so. I do not know for sure, but I always saw him with her and they were chuckling and talking ... I never knew what to say about it. And if I brought it up, then she sneered I shouldn't go 'off with the boys to drink,' and leave her there on her own."
" And who was this man?"
" His name is Antonio. He lives two blocks from here. I can't stand him, so don't say 'hi' for me."
" Okay, I think I know enough," I said. "Just one more question. Could you tell me whose blood that is on the knife in the corner?"
" Knife? What knife?"
" The knife over there."
He looked at where I was pointing and said, "Oh, that. That's just from the ... hey, you don't think that I killed my spouse with that knife, do you? I already told you I was innocent. That's just from the meat I prepared about an hour ago."
" Okay, thank you for your cooperation, Antonio. I promise you, we will hurry and resolve this case as quickly as possible."
With those words, we left the husband's workshop and walked towards Antonio's home.

Antonio was the cobbler in town. Everyone who had shoes, went to him, and it offered him a fantastic monopoly. I don't think I have to mention he was well off money-wise. I mean, nobody knew how to fix shoes other than him, and since there were almost a thousand people in town, with lots of farmers and artisans, shoes needed to be replaced a lot. But I think all of that is beside the point, because his most essential motive for the murder, the drama that had just been revealed to us, was that he was a potential cheater.

Antonio welcomed us at the door. Obviously, he had nothing else to do this afternoon, which could mean something, but I didn't want to jump to conclusions.

" Good afternoon. Come in."

Reeves and I went inside and observed the elegant place he had someone else build for him. Sapphires were on the table, along with pearls and diamonds, red drapes ornamented the walls, and the table looked like it was constructed of glass.

" Nice home," I said.

" Oh definitely. Make yourselves at home. I made everything myself. Do you want a beverage?"

" No, thank you," I said.

" Come on," he insisted.

" I will have some. Does not matter what," Reeves said.

I was okay with my partner taking a beverage from this suspect, but I had heard of a lot of poisoning tales and harmful tea circumstances to put my trust in anything liquid throughout an investigation. Antonio went to the kitchen area and came back with three beverages.

" I told you I didn't want any," I said friendly but firmly.

" Oh, I know. It's there, just in case you change your mind."

It smelled really good. "What is it?" I asked.

" It's an apple cinnamon tea mixed with some vanilla."

" Sounds wonderful," I said. "However, I am not here to talk with some hot party beverage. We understand you knew Vicky very well, and since she has just been found dead today, we are here to get to the bottom of this."

" I didn't do it," Antonio said.

" Well, we are not accusing you of anything just yet, but we do need to get some more information from you. To start with, where were you last night?"

" I was with her," he said. "I just swung by to say 'hi.' My wife said she needed some help, so I went to check if she was all right."

This guy was just lying in my face, but I expected absolutely nothing less. Naturally, his wife hadn't told him to go there. It was because he was seeing Vicky when the spouse was gone. But it didn't matter as much as his alibi, so I kept questioning him.

" And then? You went there and came home, right?"

" Uhm ... yes, that's right."

" Did she do or say anything that made you suspicious?"

" No, she was alright," he said.

" How long did you stay there?" Reeves asked.

" For about 2 hours ... uhm ... minutes I mean. I just went, talked with her for a minute or so, and after that, I left. She said one of her shoes had been ripped, so she was going to take it in today, but now that she is not here, obviously, that's not going to happen anymore. It's terrible."

This guy was so full of it, but I was still looking for hints of suspicion.

" What time did you leave?" I asked.

" I don't know. Maybe midnight."

" And your partner was fine with that?"

" Well, she didn't know about it."

" But you just said she sent you."

" Oh, did I? Well, yes, she told me about it yesterday, but I could not go because I was too busy, so I just went late at night."

" And when you went home, you ..."

" I just went to sleep."

I dug deeper. "How did you learn about the murder?"

" Well, in this town, if someone gets killed two blocks away, you pretty much find out about it," he said.

I had to confess that it sounded plausible. News spread quickly in this town. I had no further questions, so I just began some small talk till Reeves finished his drink. I stood and was about to walk out, but then I realized something. If Antonio's wife knew about him cheating with Vicky, she must have been pretty angry. This could be a motive for her to kill Vicky, just to stop her from seeing her husband ever again. When I thought of this, I turned around and said, "One more thing, Antonio."

" Yes? Anything."

" Can we talk with your spouse?"

" My spouse? No problem. She is upstairs. Can I come with you?"

" Absolutely not," I said.

" Fine. Go ahead and talk with her. I do not care. She probably knows absolutely nothing anyway."

Suspect 3: Aida

Reeves and I went up the stairs. Reeves looked at me a little surprised and asked me why I didn't want to interrogate Antonio any longer.
" His wife has more motive than he does. If he was cheating with her, then why would he kill her? It does not even make any sense. I know he was lying about a lot of things, but he doesn't appear to lie about that," I said.
" I understand," Reeves admitted.
We knocked on the door of her bedroom.
" Come in, honey," she said.
" Uhm, madam, we are not your hubby. Are you decently dressed?"
" Oh, sorry. Wait a minute."
We heard some cleaning up and some messing around going on from behind the door. I was hoping she wasn't hiding anything that had to do with the murder, for her sake, but then, if she was, our search would be over soon.
She opened the door in a brown summer gown.
" You may come in," she said as she held the door open for us. "Have a seat on the bed, gentlemen. I will be on that chair, and then you can explain me what this is all about."
We took a seat and began.
" We are in the middle of some research about the murder that has been initiated last night."
" Murder? Who got murdered?"
" Vicky, the woman that lives two blocks from you. I am a little shocked you didn't hear anything about it. Your husband did."
Her eyes were big, as if I had just announced the biggest event in history. Then a small smile appeared on her face.
" Vicky is dead?" she asked.
" Yes, she is. She was found stabbed in her chest, in her husband's bed room."
She had a difficult time restraining her feelings. It was as if she was happy this woman was finally out of her life. But she was faking it pretty well. Even Reeves was puzzled as to whether she was happy or sad.
" That's dreadful!" she exclaimed after a few fast changes of facial features. "Who did this? Who could have done this? That pitiable, wretched woman!"
" I know, Mrs. Aida. It's sad," I said calmly.
She still had a hard time not smiling, so she buried her head in her hands, concealing her face entirely. We patiently waited until she was done being psychological, either one way or the other.
" Excuse me," she said. "I am just so upset about it."
" Obviously," I said rather cynically. "Now, if you don't mind, we have a few questions for you. We just wish to know what you know. Is that alright?"
" Oh, naturally," she said.
" What do you know about Vicky?"
" Ha!" she laughed. "Not that much, except that she is the dumbest wench in the area. She hasn't even gone to school, and did I also mention that she isn't really clever? Yes, she always skipped class when I was younger, and after that she would flirt with the

boys, ALL the boys in class. I don't think it matters now, because I married a richer spouse than she did. Serves her right."

" Ahum. So she flirted with all the boys?" I asked.

" Yes, all the boys."

" Including your spouse?"

She was quiet.

Really silent.

I discovered that this was a touchy topic.

" Aida, we have reason to believe that she was cheating on her partner with your husband. What do you think of that statement?"

She was still quiet.

Then she spoke up. "He has been going there every night for the past few months. It was driving me nuts. I didn't even know what to say. I just didn't have the guts to bring it up."

" Do you understand that this gives you a motive?" I asked.

" What? You're thinking that I killed that little ...?"

She held back her words, because it appeared like she was about to swear or call the murder victim certain names.

" No!" she said. "I would never do that! I hated her, but I am not a murderer."

I calmed her down and said, "We believe you, Aida. And we feel for you, seeing the situation you're in. But just for protocol's sake, would it be alright if we searched your room for a few minutes, so we can report to the workplace that you are innocent?"

" Pfff ... Go ahead. I have absolutely nothing to hide."

We looked for a few minutes and said goodbye. If she wasn't the killer, then at least she was the happiest person to become aware of the victim going to the afterlife.

" Where are we going now?" Reeves asked as we left Antonio's and Aida's house.
" I have a number of suspects I still want to check out. The first is Vicky's uncle.
Supposedly, they were pretty close. I do not know if he has some information for us, but
I just want to make sure I am not losing out on anything important. Does that make
sense?"
" Of course," Reeves agreed.
We walked to the other side of town. It wasn't even in the area really, but barely outside,
after crossing a few roadways and farmers' lands. There it was: A giant villa fit for a
retired millionaire. It had the entire thing: Pillars, fountains, and golden decorations on
the terraces. Reeves was amazed, since he had never seen this place before.
" Whatever he did for a living, that's what I may look into," he said.
I chuckled. "Let's go talk with him, silly," I said.
We walked to the front door and knocked. An old man opened the door.
" Detective Cory," he said with a smile. "I have been expecting you."
" Good. We are here for some questioning," I said.
" I figured you would come. I heard of the murder. It's horrible."
" Uhm ... yes it is. And we are here to figure out what happened."
" Well, come in and have a seat."
The inside of the house was even better. Reeves leaned over and whispered that he
unexpectedly didn't think Antonio was wealthy anymore, compared to this guy. I
chuckled again. It was funny to notice how amazed Reeves was with all these rich
people. I could care less. I knew wealth had its enjoyment but also its problems. Once
everyone starts arguing over who gets your money, it can trigger some real awful
scenes, and I believed this millionaire's wealth might have been linked to the murder
somehow.
" Ask me anything," the old man said.
" So, Darius," I said. "You are Vicky's uncle, her mother's brother. Am I correct?"
" Yes, that's true."
" And is your sister still alive?"
" No, she died a few years ago."
" What about your wife or kids? Are any of them still alive?"
" No."
" Interesting," I said. "So after you die, who will acquire all your possessions?"
" Well, that would have been Vicky, I guess," he said. "It's all written in my will. She was
the next individual I thought of."
" And now that Vicky is dead, who will be next in line to receive what you have?"
" Oh, it's in the will too, but I don't know exactly what it says. It's been so long ago. And
perhaps if she had any children, they would be next in line, but she and Brox never had
any kids."
" So that creates a dead end, doesn't it?" I said, a little puzzled. "I am sure a lot of
people would love to have your money, but now it's unclear who will inherit it, isn't it?"
" I suppose you're right," he admitted.
" I think I know enough, Darius. Thank you for answering our questions."

We stepped outside and went back to the town. In the meantime, I spoke with my partner and told him about our next suspect, someone who had been spotted near Vicky's home during the night of the murder, a questionable figure no one in town trusted.

I made certain that Reeves was with me that late afternoon, since I was always a little terrified of going to the weird place we were going to. It was a horrible looking place, a broken home that was hardly kept up to accommodate the woman some called "the town witch." I hated going there, but I had received a report from another officer that she had been seen at the murder scene.

" Here it is," I said, pointing to the house.

" It actually gives me the shivers," Reeves said as he looked at the spikey sides of the house and black front door.

We knocked.

She opened the door.

She was frightening indeed: A woman with careless, curly hair and a brown headscarf around her neck. She was wearing big, round earrings, a lot of bracelets, and a purple dress. Behind her, there were skulls and jars with who-knows-what lined up on racks. She looked at us awkwardly.

" Yes?" she said in her squeaky voice.

" Can we come in? I am Detective Cory and this is my associate, Reeves. We want to ask you some questions about the murder that happened last night."

" Sure. I certainly do not know anything about that, but I can try to help out."

We went inside and sat down in what seemed to be the living room.

" Would you like some tea?" she asked.

" No!" Reeves unexpectedly exclaimed.

" Oh, all right. I was just offering it. Let me know if you want any. It's not a problem. I can make it in a heartbeat."

I smiled, because I realized Reeves had a harder time trusting this woman's beverages. He most likely thought her stuff was brewed in some type of cliché cauldron or something. She sat across from us and looked at us with huge eyes.

" So last night," I began, "you were found at the murder scene. Could you tell me where you were last night and what you were doing?"

" Oh, I always do my rounds," Shammy said. "I take a walk each night, just around midnight, to make certain no wicked forces are drawn to the village."

Reeves and I looked at each other. She was a pretty big weirdo, I thought, but as long as she could give us indications of the culprit, it could be valuable.

" So were you near Vicky's house yesterday?"

" Yes, I was."

" What were you doing there?"

" I felt an evil force."

" Really? Could you tell me more about that?" I asked.

" It was wicked ... EVIL I TELL YOU!"

Reeves and I flinched and leaned back as she was coming forward and waved her hands in the air. She continued, "There was an aura, a dark environment, a wicked spirit who was going to haunt this place. I didn't understand. I couldn't comprehend. There was too much. I could not stop it. Weird things ... evil hiding underneath the ether. It wouldn't disappear. Blood ... there was blood, bones, and skulls ... monsters ... ghosts ... skeletons, all over, from the underworld ..."

Her whole story became scarier than the murder itself, but I had the feeling that it was all in her head, although she may have somehow sensed something was about to occur that night. We listened to the rest and thanked her. Reeves just thought she was crazy, and I could not find any subtle clues whatsoever.

" Was anybody else there?" I finally asked.

" There were three men, just drunks, getting back from the bar," she said.

" Who were they?"

" Oh, I do not know. One of them was my ex-husband. And I felt my daughter's presence there. She is always with me. Natasha is connected to me, you see, even in her sleep."

" Sure," I said.

She did sound insane, but just to be sure, I was going to interrogate her daughter and ex-husband. We thanked her and left the house. We were both happy to be out of that place.

" Don't you think she did it?" Reeves asked.

" She hasn't left my pool of suspects yet," I answered. "But it doesn't make any sense. She is pretty insane, but she doesn't have any motive. She isn't even associated to Vicky, so if something happened between them, we 'd still have to know more about it."

Suspect 6: Natasha

Shammy's daughter was more of a pleasure to be around. We rapidly observed this to be true, even before we met her. The house was nicely constructed with charming colors and beautiful paint. The outside looked warm and inviting. It looked tiny, like any young, beginning individual would have, not like a retired millionaire or anything, but cozy nevertheless.

Her front yard was a little bit more chaotic, but that was caused by the chickens. She had about 10 chickens that were wandering around freely.

We walked past the chickens to the front door. When we knocked, she opened it and let us in. I gazed at her gorgeous appearance. She was in her early twenties, obviously, and her long, blonde hair reached down to her hips. Her peach-colored dress had something of an angelic tint to it, and her smile was to die for. If she could not help us with the case, I would make sure to visit her again sometime, that is, if she didn't have a boyfriend already.

Reeves and I took a seat and started our discussion.

" I hope we aren't invading on your personal privacy," I nicely said. "Your mother, Shammy, said she saw you outside last night. Vicky is dead, and we are looking for any clues or anybody who may more about that."

" Oh, that's fine," Natasha said. "You're fine. Yes, I was outside yesterday, but I am afraid I can't tell you much. I do not know anything about it."

" What were you doing there anyway?" I asked.

" Well," she explained, "I was very concerned about Shammy. She has become crazier lately, and the other day she was just moping around about evil spirits and dragons and such. It made no sense at all. So I silently followed her and observed her for a bit. Besides, there were some intoxicated men in the streets. I wanted to ensure she wasn't going to get in trouble with those."

" Still, it's a little odd for a girl like yourself to be up that late. Don't you think it was a little risky to follow her on your own?"

" Now that I think about it, it may not have been the brightest idea, but I definitely care about Shammy. Thankfully, nothing went wrong ... well ... except for the murder. But that was something else."

" Do you always call your mother Shammy?" I asked.

" Uhm ... yes, sometimes. She takes pride in her name. She thinks it's adorable."

I didn't know what to think about that. I thought perhaps she wasn't really proud to be Shammy's daughter, seeing that she was a little nuts, so perhaps that's why she called her by her given name. But I wasn't going to think anything without a cause.

" Your mother said her ex-husband was there. Did you see him too?"

" Yes, I think he was there. He was just partying with the guys. My dad likes to do that in the weekend, but I don't think he did anything wrong."

" Do you ever call your dad by his first name?" I asked, seeing how she referred to him in a different way.

" What? Oh, uhm ... obviously. His name is Bartholomew. If you want, you can question him too. I don't know exactly what he was doing that night, but I am sure he is not a killer."

" What makes you so sure about that?" I asked.

" Nothing specific. I just do not think he could have done it. I mean, he does not even have a motive, does he? You always need a good reason to kill somebody."
" That's very dtrue. We'll go speak to him."
We left her place, but I was sad to leave. My questions had been sharp and thorough, but inside, I felt mesmerized by her beauty and was secretly expecting something more in the future.

Suspect 7: Bartholomew

Next, we checked out Bartholomew, Natasha's dad and Shammy's ex-husband. If he was near the murder scene that night, he might have seen something and could give us some more ideas, so we could find out who had committed this crime.

Bartholomew's home was very simplistic. It looked like it came from somebody who didn't take life too seriously, at least not anymore. The exterior was good but not lavish. The door we knocked on was constructed of strong wood. But it did get opened up instantly. We heard footsteps.

" Who is it?" we heard a male voice ask.

" It's Detective Cory and Reeves. We are here to examine the murder."

It was silentl for a while.

" I didn't do it," he said.

" We know," I said, bluffing as if I actually trusted him and making him feel at ease. "But we know you were there that night, so we just would like to know what you may have seen."

" I saw absolutely nothing," was the response.

I didn't know what to say after that. I looked at my colleague. Then he stepped forward and said, "It doesn't matter. We still want to come in. If you don't let us in, we'll come back with a warrant. Would you rather have that?"

Then we heard a ton of clicks. It sounded like he just opened a dozen locks. Very suspicious individual, this Bartholomew character. He glimpsed around the corner of his door and said, "Okay, come in, quickly."

We stepped in and sat down on one of the chairs in his simplified living-room. He sat across from us and revealed a certain worry in his eyes. I do not know if this was typical, or if he got even more skittish after what had happened last night, but I started.

" We would just like to know what you were doing last night and if you saw anything," I said.

" I was just at the bar and walked through the streets with my 2 friends," he said. "I saw my ex-wife there. She was sitting down on her knees and throwing her hands up in the air, chanting some unusual spells of some sort. That woman keeps creeping me out. Why do you think I got a divorce?"

" Ah, yes. But we're not here to ask you about your previous marriage," I said. "We are just looking for hints. What else did Shammy do?"

" She patted her hands on the floor and then cursed the gods for allowing evil upon us. Then she went home and made some other odd sounds. I didn't stick around for too long, because I didn't want to be humiliated in front of the people."

" Did you see Natasha there?"

" My daughter? Was she there? I didn't see her. What was she doing outside that late?"

" Perhaps following her insane mother who was chanting spells and making noises," I said.

" Oh, but Shammy is not her mother," Bartholomew said.

" Excuse me?"

" Shammy is not Natasha's mother," he repeated. "I am her father, but Shammy is her stepmother. She always despised her. That's why she won't ever see her."

" I am sorry? Did you just say that she will not ever see her? But she said she was following Shammy that night because she was concerned," I said.

" That doesn't sound right," Bartholomew said. "She has always been bitter towards her real mother because she dumped her with me and that freak."

" Okay, all right," I said. "It's starting to make a little bit more sense now. Could you enlighten us with some more information about your family structure, please?"

" Certainly. You see, when Vicky and I broke up, she was already pregnant with Natasha. But when Natasha was born, she handed her to me, saying she didn't have the means to look after her. Natasha matured in this house, with me and Shammy, but she always disliked her. Additionally, she hated her own mother much more. She kept it a secret, but I knew how bitter she was when she discovered that Vicky was her mother and had disposed her to be raised by Shammy."

A light bulb lit up in my brain. It seemed so far-fetched. Vicky did have a daughter, but she never told anybody about her. Natasha would get all her great-uncle's riches, and since she had always despised her real mother for deserting her, she just became a suspect with 2 motives.

Reeves was paying close attention to Bartholomew's story. He was beginning to connect the dots too. When we left, we entered into a street to discuss the matter.

The Murderer

" Do you really think a young, stunning woman like that would kill her own mother?" Reeves asked me.

" It's too bad that she is young and beautiful," I confessed. "But she has 2 reasons for doing so: The hate for her mother Vicky, who abandoned her and put her with that odd woman, and the inheritance of her great-uncle. There is no doubt in my mind she is the one who did it."

" And what about proof?" Reeves asked.

" Let me think," I said.

I thought.

And thought.

" Aha!" I all of a sudden screamed. "I've got it! The feather I saw! The chickens! It all makes sense now. The feather I found at the murder scene came from Natasha's chicken cage. But we need more. Let's go. You get the police and I will go to her home."

" Uhm ... I do not know if that's such a good idea," he objected. "If she is a killer, then you should not go there on your own."

" We do not want her to get away either, do we?" I asked.

" No, of course we don't."

" Okay, then I will stay outside, in front of her house, just to ensure she doesn't come out."

" That seems like a better plan," he agreed.

I ran towards Natasha's home with a heavy heart, feeling the sadness for such a tragedy and drama. If she truly was the killer, then one life had already been destroyed by all the working circumstances. It was terrible. Besides, now there would not be a future for me with that sexy girl any longer, so perhaps that's also a loss I lamented a little.

I stood there and waited for the police. When a few officer came, we all went to the door and barged in. We looked everywhere, and eventually, we found a knife set, one of which was most likely the murder weapon. But Natasha was gone.

" Go to the backdoor!" I commanded.

Reeves and another officer hurried outside.

" There she is!" he said.

All of us pursued her. We saw her zigzagging through the narrow village streets, trying to avoid her accusers, but it was useless. One of the officers cut her off and got her.

" It wasn't my fault! It was all my mom's fault! She deserted me! It wasn't fair! She was never there for me!" she screamed as she got caught and cuffed.

She was then taken to prison, and after a trial, more proof was found. On the one hand, I was happy that the case got resolved; on the other hand, I felt a little sorry for her.

Was her hate for her mother her biggest motive, or was it the greed for her great-uncle's treasures? I thought we would never completely comprehend it, but obviously, she had already been a victim of life since her childhood. This was the part I disliked about my job: Seeing all the mental harm triggered by people every day.

It became clear again, something I had always contemplated, that we often become aware of crimes and wars, but that the real drama, the hidden feelings and the hurt, are right below the surface. The biggest defects of society are those that aren't always visible till something drastic occurs.

I stood there, staring at her charming home one more time. I saw the chickens, which would soon be confiscated by the state. I thought of the warm interior where we had such an enjoyable discussion. It was sad.

" Let it go," Reeves said as he put his arm around my shoulder. "Someday, she may be healed. There is still hope. Do not worry. And there is still hope for you too."

I smiled. good old Reeves, always there to cheer me up.

" Thanks, partner," I said silently.

We left and went to the police bureau. Who knew what else I was going to run into? On to the next case ...

THE END

Writings on the Wall

My name is Dorus. I am from a tranquil town. I am 31 and my parents live far from here. Nothing ever takes place here. Everyone goes through the regular routine of the day. They do their job, they play with their families, and they go to bed with their marriage partners. Nothing out of the ordinary.

Or so it appears ...

One day, I got up. The roosters in this town made sure of that. I also enjoyed the sound of singing birds each day, which appear early each day, beside my window. Oh, and I am not the kind of person who has a difficult time rising early, because if I try to sleep in, another animal makes sure I don't stay in my nest for too long.

Rudolph is my dog. Yes, I named him after a reindeer, but he's a dog. Just accept it. He is a German Shepherd, and he is big. I love him to pieces. He is the best friend I've ever had. Well, not that I do not have any friends whatsoever, but Rudolph is there for me.

We go to the park and play fetch; I pet him when I don't know what to do with my hands, and I talk with him when I am lonely.

But just recently, we were outside, just walking around, when Rudolph sniffed and began barking unexpectedly.

" Bark! Bark!"

" What's going on, Rudolph?"

" Bark! Bark! Bark!" he barked.

Then he ran into a different direction. I ran after him, wondering what all the fuss was about. Then I saw it.

Oh my goodness! It was a corpse!

A big man was lying behind a dumpster, bathing in his own blood, and looking as if he was cut up or bitten somehow. I came a little closer and tried to see who it was. I covered my mouth in awe.

It was Josh!

How could anyone kill Josh? Firstly, he was the best guy ever, and also, he was so big and strong that it could have taken something extremely strong to take him down.

It didn't take long before other villagers were gathering around the victim. The town police came and took control of the scene, and a few of the villagers began talking.

" Who could have done this?"

" I bet it was his neighbor. He was always envious of him."

" Yes, but to kill him? You can't just start accusing people of murder. Besides, that would be gossiping."

" Gossiping? I am just trying to find out who did it. I am just brainstorming."

I was listening intently to all these conversations and presumptions. It worried me. If there was a killer in our village, we wouldn't be safe anymore. And we had no clue whom to blame.

But this was only the beginning ...

In that same week, 3 more murders occurred: Two more men and one woman. They were gruesome, and I am thankful that I only found out about them, because finding another dead body would have been traumatic.

No one knew, and everyone was thinking about it. People were playing the blame game in our town. They turned against each other and accused others a lot. The whole environment changed. It wasn't pleasant.

Chapter 2: The Inscriptions

With the aura that was cast over this town, people were afraid to go outside in the dark. They didn't trust it. The murderer was out there someplace, and I couldn't blame them for wanting to not be the next victim.

So yes, I remained inside too, specifically when the sun went down. But one night, I just couldn't take it. I had been inside a lot, and I discovered that Rudolph was already peeing in the house. So I thought it was time to take him for a walk. I took a knife from the cooking area and put it in my pocket, just in case anyone would try to assault me. Rudolph and I walked through the streets. There was an eerie fog in the air; it actually gave me the chills. I didn't like the fact that I could not see farther than a half block away. It was gloomy and obscure.

Rudolph didn't care, though. He was having a blast, finally having the chance to go outside and all. He peed in one corner, sniffed another, and ran towards the next street all the time, making me lose sight of him.

" Rudolph, stay here please. Rudolph!"

He was gone. I was all by myself. I hated this. I even grabbed the knife in my pocket and looked around. I knew the way, but I sort of appreciated him for directing me. Where did he go?

And then I heard, "Bark! Bark!"

" Rudolph?"

I could not see anything. That stupid fog ... ughh ...

" Bark! Bark!"

I saw from which direction it was coming, so I took some courage and moved along, looking for my huge German Shepherd.

" Ah, there you are," I said after a few minutes. "Don't flee from me anymore. I do not want to be alone with these things happening in town. What are you barking at anyway?"

I looked at the wall he was barking at.

" Whoa" was all I could say.

It was the craziest think I had ever seen, and it was another clue to the puzzle. The wall was nothing else but a normal wall, but on it, there were names written. Some of them were sculpted, and others were painted, but there were real names on there. And not just any names ... the EXACT names of the people who had been murdered!

" Are you thinking what I am thinking?" I asked my pet.

" Bark! Bark!"

" That's what I thought. These were either written after the murders, to keep an eye on who got killed ... or ..." I shivered for a moment. ".. or they were written before the murders to indicate who was going to die."

" Bark!"

" I know, I know. I will tell the police about it tomorrow. Let's go home. This place gives me the creeps."

After that, we went home.

The next day, I woke up by the noise of birds. I was curious to discover more about the mystical wall with the names, so I got some food, took my dog, and headed out the door.
" Let's go, Rudolph," I said.
We went to the other side of town, where we had seen the names on the wall. When we arrived, the names were still there.
" Ha! You see? There is Josh, and Melissa, and Roland, and Nery, and ..."
I paused.
I could not believe my eyes.
" ... and Dorus," I said quietly.
" Bark! Bark!" Rudolph said.
My face became pale. My heart was beating quicker. A million ideas went through my mind within seconds, but they all came down to the same thing: I was going to die. What?! Why was my name on there? I wasn't dead. I had absolutely nothing to do with these victims. What was going on here? This was getting scarier by the minute.
Was I going to die? But by whom? And how?
For a few minutes, the worry beset my very being. I was drenched in agonizing anxiety and dreadful terror. But then my survival instincts kicked in. I was going to prevent this! I wasn't dead YET! And who was to say that I couldn't change my supposed fate?
I was determined, eager to go and solve the puzzle, and to prevent my own death.
I rushed home and took a few of the brushes and magnifying glasses from my cabinet. These tools could help me establish who had been writing these names on the wall.
Just a side note: If this was some kind of sick joke, then it certainly wasn't amusing.
After grabbing the tools, I ran back to the wall. Rudolph followed me there. I was looking through the magnifying glass and then I brushed off a little dust, wanting to discover the products being used and maybe some other things that would lead me to the perpetrator.
But then Rudolph barked again.
" Bark! Bark!"
" What is it, Rudolph?"
I looked behind me and saw a shady figure run behind another home. Hey, what was that individual doing here? Was I being watched?
" Let's get him, Rudolph!" I said.
And the chase started.

Chapter 4: The Cave We Found

With my dog, I chased after the shady figure through the streets of my hometown. It was extremely early in the morning, so even in this village, there was no one else up yet. Everyone was still sleeping, which was a downer, because this meant I had to do it all by myself.

Of course, Rudolph was a lot faster than I was, but for some reason, this suspect was lightning fast as well.

When we came to the town's border, the shady figure was far in the distance, on the other side of a large farm field. How he arrived so rapidly was a secret to me. But I didn't give up, and neither did Rudolph.

" Let's keep going!" I told my pet dog. "But stay with me. I don't want to lose you."

I ran as fast as I could, and Rudolph made certain he didn't get ahead of me too much. He was such a great dog. I love him. At the end of the field, went into a forest at the foot of a mountain. I instantly saw all the wood and the ore in the ground that we could use to build more in the town, but I wasn't sure if the villagers knew anything about all these products and building rocks. Anyway, if I would return, I would tell them about it.

Listen to me ... saying if I would return ... I wasn't really going to die, was I? No. That should be: when I would return, I would tell them about it. I was going to stop this from occurring.

After walking through the small forest, I saw a small cave in the mountain. I presumed the dubious figure was hiding in there. And when I would find him, I would beat the answers right out of him, because this was getting outrageous.

The cave was dark, but there were a few torches on the walls, that made me understand that this person had been living here all this time. With Rudolph, I snuck into the main space of the cave, where I saw what had been observing me near the wall.

Chapter 5: Black Magic in the Cave

It was a witch!
I didn't know a witch lived here.
The witch had a weird nose, purple clothes, and a black hat. She was dancing around a cauldron, not realizing that I had followed her all the way down here. She must have presumed I had given up, which benefitted me at the time.
The cavern had all kinds of things in it. Torches were burning on the walls, and axes, magic rocks and pearls were lying around on the ground.
This place was a mess.
I covered my nose when I smelled the reeking odor that emanated from the cauldron, and looked in disgust at the rats that were munching on pieces of cardboard, and the cockroaches I saw hiding in the corners of this rank place. Decomposing apples and a half-eaten fish were covered by mold and flies, and some sort of fluid acid had been spilled all over the place, triggering the floor to be rather uneven by the holes it had burned here and there. It was an awful sight, this messy, disorderly cave. She certainly didn't know anything about house cleaning, but then again, maybe she just didn't care.
Rudolph was growling a little.
" Sssshhh ..." I whispered. "Let's just see what she does."
As the witch was jumping around, she took a little pepper here or another bottle of vinegar there, and tossed the stuff into the boiling substance in the cauldron. I didn't truly care what she was making, though. I wasn't liking this for one bit. The thought crossed my mind that she was going to poison me with this liquid stuff.
I watched as she stirred and stirred, added in other components, and laughed with an evil, squeaky voice.
" Eeeh-heee-heee!"
" Typical for a witch," I thought.
Then Rudolph barked.
" Bark! Bark!"
The witch turned our way. "Oh, you were just the one I was trying to find!" she yelled.
" You evil monster ... you were going to kill me, weren't you?"
" I am still going to kill you, Dorus, and that dumb dog of yours too."
" I do not understand. What did I do to you?"
" Oh, it's very easy to understand," the witch said. "I've been living in this impoverished cave all my life. Nobody cared about me, and no one gave me anything to hang in there. But I will now give them something to be terrified about. Perhaps now they will begin caring."
" But that does not make any sense. What are you trying to accomplish by eliminating the villagers?"
" Fear," she said. "If they become so scared that they don't have the guts to leave their homes, they will eventually all leave. And when they do, I am going to live there. Heeheehee! All their houses and structures will be MINE!!!"
" So all you're attempting to do, is terrifying them off so you can move in there? That just sounds dumb. And moreover, I. won't ... let you."
" Don't be too positive, young guy. I may be old, but I know what I am doing. Here, take this ..."

She ducked and grabbed an explosive potion. I chuckled and said, "Pfff ... you're going to give me a drink or something?"

Then she tossed it. It blew up!

Booooooooom!

Luckily, it exploded in front of me, and I had just had enough time to dive behind a rock. What the ... what was that? Some kind of Molotov cocktail or something? This witch was crazy, throwing explosive potions and stuff.

" Here, take another one," she said as she threw another.

Boooooom!

Another explosion. She missed again. Ha! But what was I going to do? I had to stop this wicked witch from exterminating the villages until they would leave.

" Rudolph!" I screamed. "Go get her!"

Rudolph didn't need far more to hear from me. He knew what I meant. This witch was throwing stuff at me, and he wasn't liking it more than I did.

" Bark! Bark! Bark!" Rudolph said as he stormed at the witch. He jumped at her and pinned her to the floor.

" Aaarhghgh! That silly dog of yours!"

I came out of my hiding spot, and ran at her. I had her. I finally had her, and she wasn't going anywhere.

" You think you won?" she said. "You haven't seen anything yet. Why do you think I wrote those names on the wall? I am going to summon the monster that devoured the others, and there is no escaping it. Hahaha!"

The witch pushed the dog away and rapidly jumped to some sand she had in the corner. She put the sand into a T-shape and placed three skeleton skulls on top of the three rocks. The last rock was a skeleton skull.
And after that, it happened.
It grew bigger and bigger. Before I knew it, a big skeleton stood before me, gnashing its teeth and sort of imploding or something.
The skeleton had 3 big heads and sharp teeth. Its piercing eyes looked directly at me.
" Aaaah!" I screamed as I ran from the cavern. Rudolph followed me, and so did my enemy. I hid behind a tree, panting heavily because of my previous quick sprint. I saw Rudolph, but was the skeleton still there?
Had that witch just been writing random names on the wall, and after that summoning the skeleton to send it out to kill them? That's what it looked like at least.
Anyway, I had to focus again. It didn't matter for now, because in the meantime, this beast was still following me. I looked, with my head peeking around the tree trunk. Yep, it was still there, and getting closer and closer.
Then I looked at Rudolph.
I looked at the tree.
I had an idea. I bent over and picked up a branch from the ground and said, "Hey, Rudolph. Do you want to play fetch?"
" Bark! Bark!" Rudolph said. These were good barks. I could tell, because he had a big smile on his face and his tail was wagging.
" Then go play fetch!" I said, as I tossed the stick towards the skeleton.
Rudolph didn't wait on anything to occur. He sped at the skeleton and jumped right through the bones towards the stick, spreading the wicked enemy's bones all over the ground. I ran towards them and looked at it. The bones were slowly coming together, as if the skeleton tried to regroup or something. But then I had another idea.
" Rudolph, Rudolph! Do not be pleased with the stick. Just get the bone!"
I picked up one of the skeleton's bones and tossed it into the distance. Rudolph happily ran after it and started to chew on it. And me? I kicked the skulls over and crushed a few of the bones with my foot. Others I banged against the tree trunk to break them in half. It all seemed to work.
The skeleton didn't get up anymore. The risk was over. The triumph was mine!
Oh, wait, but what about the witch?
" Let's get her, Rudolph!" I said, but Rudolph didn't want to release the bone. He was having the time of his life chewing at that thing.
" Come on, pet dog. You can take the bone with you. No worries."
Ultimately, he just picked it up and followed me, particularly since he saw that I was leaving without him. We ran inside and there she was, standing prepared with another explosive potion. "I wondered if you would be smart enough to beat my skeleton," she said. "But now, I am going to blow you up with this potion. Say goodbye! Heeheeheeeee!"
She tossed the potion at me, but those things only blow up when they hit the ground. I guess, now that I look at it, that I owe my life to my pet, because at that specific

moment, Rudolph jumped up and caught the potion, preventing it from hitting the ground.

" Good boy!" I said. "Now give it to me."

But Rudolph wouldn't let go. He was having too much fun.

" Let go, release that thing ... down, boy."

We pulled and pulled, and eventually, I was able to rip it from his teeth. I looked at the witch and squinted my eyes.

" This is for the villagers you murdered," I said in a low voice.

I threw the potion back, which flew through the air and hit the ground right in front of the wicked witch.

" Nooooooo!" she screamed. But it was far too late. The potion blew up in her face, causing the cave ceiling to break, after which big boulders fell on the witch and crushed her. Huge vapors of smoke vaporized from the scene, and I waved a few of it away with my hand, coughing in the meantime.

I looked.

The witch was gone.

There died the witch.

She had been buried beneath the rocks from the cave. Ironically, the home she so desperately tried to leave, became her tomb.

I hugged my dog. It was remarkable just how much Rudolph had helped me in this experience. Then I took one more appearance and returned to the village.

Chapter 7: Safe

Back at the town, a massive crowd is awaiting me. Well, as big as a crowd from my town can get, I should say. Maybe a few hundred people ... perhaps less. But suffice it to say that most of the villagers had gathered at the main square and were welcoming me back.

" We were worried," one of the women said.

" You were gone for such a long time," a man said. "We were afraid that you were the next victim. Besides, my son said he saw your name on the wall with the other victims. What is going on here?"

I smiled. I felt right at home, seeing that the other villagers cared so much about me. I looked at my pet and at the multitude. They were all staring at me, waiting on a description.

" Well?" one of them said.

" Uhm ..." I began. "I do not know if you even need to know everything that happened in that forest, and in the cave."

" What is that?"

" Never mind."

I hesitated for a moment. Should I tell them about the witch, the skeleton, and the potions? Perhaps that would only scare them, knowing that such things existed in or near their town. There were kids staring at me too. One little girl even came to me and asked, "Mister, did you die?"

" No, I didn't die," I said with a happy face. "I came close to death, but all is well now." Then I said the following, "Listen, everyone, I will tell you these three things: Number one, whatever or whoever it was that murdered our fellow citizens is gone. That person will never bother us again. So please, feel free to go out during the night again and stop being afraid. Number 2, I don't think you have any idea just how much wood and ore there is outside your town. If a few of you want to explore some in that direction, please let me know and I will definitely like to guide you there. And number 3 ..."

I raised Rudolph above me, putting the faithful but heavy German Shepherd on my shoulders.

" ... Umpf ... number three is that Rudolph saved my life ... and the village. If anybody deserves to be honored, it is him."

All the villagers looked astonished. A few of them were attempting to understand what I was describing, but others just cheered.

" Hooray for Rudolph! Hooray for Dorus and Rudolph!"

What followed later on, was a giant banquet to which the whole village was invited. People felt safe again. They were assured that no one would die anymore. The joyful environment of peace had been returned.

And Rudolph?

He received a whole bowl filled with bones and meat for himself. He deserved it.

THE END

The Hoody

Chapter 1: Turned down for the First Time

It is clear that a lot of the young women in my class do not like me. I mean, they gossip about everything. They dislike my green jacket, my skirt, and especially my hoody. Well, they're not so perfect either, but let's not talk about that. I preserve my own style, if you will, something I have always been proud of.

I am Carissa, and I am 21 years old. Do you know how people are to each other at that age? They're mean! It's because they are trying to become more popular, and one of the best ways, they think, is by putting somebody else down. I never wanted to take part in that silly social game. I just sort of did my own thing.

That's not to say that I was normal. Other ladies didn't wear hoodies. They didn't wear green. In fact, a ton of them wore pinks and purples, just to appear more feminine. Not me. I was a green girl, and let me tell you why. You most likely already saw it coming. I love green beasts; that's the reason.

Ha! How can anybody love them, right? They're horrible, filthy, and ... well ... creepy. But I think I saw something in these sophisticated creatures that no one else did. I drew green beasts, I was always talking about them, I read books about them, and I was astonished at the way they could run fast and explode out of the blue. Their self-destructive tendencies were confusing to me, but maybe they just had those because they weren't too clever in the first place. It was just their nature.

Our village mainly consisted of farmers. Some of them were wise, others appeared to be foolish in my eyes.

Anyway, even if they are farmers, does not mean that some of them aren't exceptionally good-looking. That was one of my weaknesses: My dad was always gone and I think I was searching for that male role model in my life, so I drew closer to the boys in school, which weren't always mature enough, I have to say. But every once in a while, I would have a crush on one of them and go wild over a particular guy.

The first one was named Malcolm. His character? Well, from observing him, I knew he liked to play sports, soccer in a special way. He also smelled fantastic when he came out of the locker room (yes, that was me being odd by watching him). And he socialized with a few of the popular guys. Was he out of my league? I didn't know. I didn't notice those things extremely well, so I knew there was only one way to find out. I needed to just go for it.

But my strategy had to be perfect. I didn't want to humiliate myself in front of my peers, and being turned down was something that would have such an impact. The very first time, I didn't get it. I didn't comprehend guys, and between you and me, I do not think they comprehend themselves at that age either. I was too forward. I was too eager. I should have been subtler.

So one day, I just walked up towards Malcolm in the corridor, when he was standing beside the lockers with his friends, and I said, "I like you. Will you be my partner?" Wrong move. Ladies, don't ever do this. You have to build it up first, which was a significant mistake I made.

All he did, was stop talking with his macho friends, whom I didn't especially like, by the way. Then he looked at me and asked, "Who are you again?"

" I am Carissa," I said from underneath my hoody, and shaking with anxiety.

" Carissa? Well, Carissa, I don't know anything about you, and since you're hiding your face, you must not be that pretty. Besides, I already like someone else. So thanks for the offer, but the answer is 'no.'"

" Oh, all right," I said shyly, and after that I walked away.

Some girls in the same hallway laughed. Now they had another thing to chatter about. Great. And the next day, after crying for the entire evening, I saw a ton of students staring at me. Some of them laughed, and others were just looking.

What a dumb choice I had made!

Chapter 2: Rejected Again and Again

The next crush was 2 months later. I had not discovered Jack before, since he went to a different class. I had locked my heart for a while and thrown away the key, but when I saw him, I could not get over how much I was attracted to him. His wavy, blond hair matched his large t-shirt and his blue eyes perfectly. He was a stud! I wanted him to be my sweetheart so we could kiss and ... well, you know the rest.

Nevertheless, this time, I was prepared. I wouldn't make the same mistake again. I would just wrap him around my finger. I went to the bathroom and got ready. I put my best makeup on. I loosened my hair, and despite the fact that red-heads weren't popular in school, I knew I could make myself pretty if I did my best. And this time, I would eliminate the green beast jacket. I took a pink tang top and a red skirt. Lipstick, eye shadow, and some huge, round earrings would finish the job. I put on some elegant boots I had purchased with my allowance money, and I went for it.

I was subtle this time. All I did, was walk by him, smile, and say, "Hi, Jack."

He waved back, a little baffled but still flattered.

That same afternoon, I sat a little closer to him during lunch break and tried to start a conversation. "I've noticed you," I said. "You are in a different class, but I see you in the corridor every once in a while."

" I saw you today," he said. "What's your name?"

" Carissa."

" Good to meet you, Carissa. How old are you?"

" I am 21," I said. "You?"

" I am 26. Well, good to speak to you, but I have to go."

And that's when I became a little afraid. How else was I going to approach him? I didn't know what to do, so when he stood, I said, "Wait. Do you think you and I can go study at the library at some point ... you know ... together ... to understand our homework assignment better?"

He thought for a moment and then said, "Look, Carissa. I like your friendliness, but the important things I study, are way more complicated than what I got in your class. I don't think you would be much help to me."

He was about to leave, so I made another desperate attempt, but I wasn't watching myself, so I said, "I love you."

Oh no. Oh no! Did I just say that? Did those words come out of my mouth? No, no, no, no, no! He was going to think I was insane! Why couldn't I manage my words? Bad Carissa, bad! What now?

" You're a sweet girl, Carissa," he said, "but I typically do not date women who are that eager. No offense. All the best with your homework though."

Noooo! I got declined again! And the worst of it all was that I couldn't even dislike him for it. He was a great guy! He wasn't even impolite to me! Ugggh ... another embarrassment. Thankfully, nobody saw it that time, and Jack was so great that he didn't even tell anybody about it. So he saved me the pain of becoming the school's gossip topic for the next few days.

Thanks, Jack, but then again, thanks for nothing. Another broken heart. I was devastated, but I didn't cry as much as the very first time. Fortunately, I had become a bit stronger by then.

Chapter 3: This Was It

Because of the previous rejections, I became even more careful in my methods. Actually, I wasn't trying too much any longer. I just let it happen. Obviously, it didn't, because what boy would be attracted to a girl in a green beast attire with a hoody? One day, though, I was sitting on a bench during lunchbreak. I was eating my peanut butter sandwich and drinking from a bottle of water.
" I like your hoody," someone said.
I looked up.
" Huh?"
" Your hoody; I like it," the boy standing next to me said.
He wasn't as masculine and fit as my previous crushes, and he was wearing glasses. In fact, he looked like a wimp, but at least I was going to be respectful.
" Thank you," I said. "Most people don't. Why do you like it?"
" I do not know," he said. "Perhaps it reminds me of green beasts, the 2nd most wanted monsters on earth, the only ones that can blow up and have the determination to give up their own lives when they need to."
I couldn't believe my ears! A boy who liked those monsters as well!
" Fascinating creatures, aren't they?" I confirmed.
" Indeed, they are. I read about them the other day, and I could not help but think that they are the most advanced creatures on earth."
" Really? I see it the same way. That's why I wear this jacket."
" Can you remove your hoody?" he asked.
" Why?"
" I just want to see your hair better. You have a pretty face."
" Sure," I said, although I wasn't certain about it. My self-esteem was low at that moment; besides, I didn't want to be vulnerable. I doubted, but I did it because he asked so well.
" Oh, you have red hair," he said. Apparently, he had not seen my hair before.
I didn't like his response. I was offended. Did he not like my red hair? Was this character another one of those boys who was only searching for blondes? Fine, if he didn't want me, just because of my hair color, then that was it! The other guys didn't like me either. I wasn't going to try again. Love stinks.
After all these ideas, in a few seconds, I put my hoody back on, got my lunch, and began to leave.
" Wait!" he said. "Why are you leaving? Was it something I said?"
I didn't react. I had HAD it. I was so done with this twenties relationship drama thing. Perhaps I would try again at the age of 29 or 30, or better yet, maybe I would just choose to stay single. There!
I returned to class and tried to pay attention to the instructors' lessons, but it was too difficult. I felt declined again. I didn't want anything to do with guys ever again!

Chapter 4: Enough! Enough Already!

I was actually upset that afternoon. I went to my house and hid my face below my hoody as much as possible. I didn't want to talk to anyone, specifically not Antonio. What an insult! He hated my red hair, like everyone else. Well, I wasn't going to die it. Take it or leave it, stupid guys!

I came home and greeted my mom. Then I went directly to my room. As I was packing a couple of things and filling my backpack with some snacks, a blanket, and my toothbrush, my mother entered my room and asked me what was wrong.

" I am leaving," I said. "I have had it with this town."

" Please stay," my mother said. "You can't simply leave like that. We love you. What is going on? Take a seat and describe to me why you're so upset."

" No. Let me go!" I said.

" Carissa, please. Just breathe and take a minute." She got me by my shoulders and looked into my eyes.

I gave in. I sat down on my bed and sobbed, "Nobody likes me."

" That's not really true," my mom said. "I like you, and your father likes you. I am quite sure there are kids at school who like you too."

" The ladies hate me. They gossip about me. And the boys ... well, whenever I have a crush on someone, I get declined."

" Ah, some guy issues, huh?" my mom said. "I recall having those."

" It was simple for you, mom," I said. "You have blond hair. But because my dad has red hair, I acquired red hair. It's not fair!"

" Ha! You're a poet and you don't really know it," my mother said.

I stared at her in a mean way.

" S-sorry. Please continue," she said.

" Well, today it just happened again," I went on. "There is this dude who was a little into me, and as soon as I took off my hoody, he said that he hated my red hair."

" He truly said that? Literally?"

" Uhm ... it was implied, actually," I said. "However, who cares? I don't wish to go to school anymore."

" You are in luck, kiddo. It's weekend, so tomorrow, you can stay home or go into town with me. Wouldn't that be fun?"

" Sorry, mom, but I am too old to go market shopping with my mother. The other kids will laugh at me if I do that."

" Okay, suit yourself," she said. "Know that I am here for you if you need me." Then she left the bedroom.

I thought about what she said, and yet I was a stubborn young woman. 3 rejections were enough for me to understand that I wasn't wanted. Besides, I wanted to leave the town anyhow. For that reason, I kept the important things in my bag and waited until the evening. When the night came, I snuck out. I tiptoed through the town streets and entered into the forest. It was dark and weird, but I loved the adventurous taste I was having. As I kept going through the woods, I saw all the owls, the rats, and some other wild animals there. It was as if they wouldn't reveal themselves in the daytime, and as if they liked my guts right there and then.

I kept walking for a couple of hours and reached a cave at the foot of the mountain. I looked for predators, but there were none.

" This appears like a comfortable area," I said.

I pulled the blanket out of my backpack and sat down. The fresh air and the darkness of the night were excellent for an open-air slumber party.

" I don't care if they try to find me or not," I said to myself. "I am going to be right here. Tomorrow, maybe I'll select some berries to eat."

Chapter 5: Chasing Me

This is Antonio. Carissa enabled me to compose this one chapter in her journal, so it would make more sense, and to discuss what happened a little better. To put it simply, to fill in the blanks of what occurred in between her previous notes and the next ones. When I talked with her at school, she appeared distraught over my comment about her hair. However, I wasn't even done talking yet. I loved her hair! I had actually always liked red hair. It was a secret I had actually never ever exposed to anyone, so, yes, when she removed her hoody, I said, "Oh, you have red hair!" As delighted as I was, I attempted to constrain myself, and maybe that sent the wrong message.

However, this journal Part has to do with the next day: Saturday. I was up early. Something informed me that Carissa was in trouble o some sort. An intuition maybe? Or something else? I didn't know what it was, and yet I went to her house. By the way, because this town is little enough that practically everybody understands everybody, it didn't take me long to find out where she lived.

I knocked on the door. I waited. After some time, her mother opened up.

" Yes?" she said.

" Is Carissa here?" I asked.

" No, she is not. She has actually run away from the house. We are worried. I have been looking all over town and am simply waiting here for the cops to get here."

" Okay. I know enough," I said.

She ran away from the house? Where could she have gone? And at that exact moment, I became determined to go find her. But not long after that, I would have another reason ...

" Alaaaaaarm!" a messenger yelled as he ran around in the peaceful streets of our little farmers' town. "We are being assaulted!"

At that moment, a policeman walked around the corner and stopped him. "Whoa, wait a minute, boy. Who is being attacked? Who is assaulting us?"

" Gr-green beasts," the man said while panting. "There is a whole army of them on the other side of the hill. Probably hundreds. I just returned from that part. There is no chance we can stand up to them."

I was a little confused. Here I was, after returning from Carissa's house, and suddenly, a policeman and a messenger were telling each other that the whole town was now in danger. What was I going to do?

" What are we going to do?" the police officer asked.

" I don't know," the man said. "I am simply here to deliver you the message. I am taking my household out of here. If those beasts blow up my home, then at least we won't perish in it."

I got sidetracked by my own ideas. Now it wasn't just a matter of seeing Carissa and asking her to come back. I had to warn her! But really, where could she be?

Funny enough, a ton of villagers had mentioned the mountain cavern. It was the first place that came up in my mind. Where else would she be able to find shelter? Besides, it rained often in our green, moist environment, so I was sure that I had a great chance of finding her there.

And off I went, wishing to run into her.

Chapter 6: This Is Just Me

This is Carissa once again, simply continuing my journal. I got up by the noise of birds chirping. The woods were an excellent place to find some solitude. I stretched my arms and legs, looked around, and bent over. One of the worries was about my mom and dad got shoved aside in my mind, and I watched the sunrays through the trees. It was gorgeous in this nature location.

I scavenged for berries, and encountered a big raspberry bush.

" Jackpot," I said. "This is what I wanted for breakfast. Perhaps I need to return here with my mom and dad at some point and get all the ones that are left after I consume these."

Saying that, I recognized that I ought to go home again. There was no point in staying upset. And my mom and dad hadn't done anything wrong. It was just my own feelings getting in my way. Life is odd.

Anyhow, after checking out the forest a bit more, I unexpectedly heard somebody scream my name.

" Carissa! Carissa!"

Who could that be?

I ran towards the noise and was shocked to see the exact same geeky kid that I liked the day before "Antonio?" I said. "What are you doing here?"

" I could ask you the same question, but I'll go first. I came here to find you."

" I escaped. I was distressed."

" Why?".

" It's none of your business, actually," I said. I didn't want to open up.

" Is it because I said something about your hair? I never said I disliked it."

Wow. This Antonio kid was a little nerdy, yet he was compassionate, and he knew what I was feeling. Score! I liked him again.

" I like red hair," he said. "In fact, I was usually searching for a lady with red hair."

" Really?".

" Really."

" Then let's go to the house together."

I was quite sure that from that time on, we were boyfriend and girlfriend, due to the fact that he grabbed my hand and held throughout the forest.

" There is something else," he said. "The town remains in turmoil. Everyone is afraid. A big army of explosive beasts is coming our way, and I don't understand what to do about it. Have you ever read anything about how to stop them?".

" Are you kidding me? I know all about them," I said. "And I don't think that anybody else knows about these little secrets. Believe me, Antonio, I am a real green beast lady. I have met some monsters before, and I understand precisely what to do."

" Cool. I just knew you had it in you," he said. "You're fantastic."

I blushed and said, "Let's go before it is far too late."

Chapter 7: Monsters

The two of us ran towards the village. It was regrettable, yet we needed to release each other's hands to do so. I actually thought it was amusing that I ran faster than Antonio, and also that I got home right before he did.

" Are we going to your house or my mine?" he asked.

" Mine, naturally," I said.

" Oh, okay."

I didn't knock when we showed up. I stormed in and searched for my mom and dad.

" Mom!" I screamed.

" Carissa ?!" I heard from upstairs. "Carissa, is that you?".

" Yes, mother. I am at the house. I am sorry I left, but I am alright."

" I am so glad you're back," my mother said as she came downstairs and gave me a big hug. "We were worried about you."

" I'm alright, mother. You can let go now. Did you hear about the green beasts?".

" Yes, I did. We need to leave as soon as possible."

" No, mother, we do not," I said.

" What is this? Why won't you come?".

" I can resolve it. I can make the monsters disappear."

" Look, Carissa. I understand you like green beasts and also that you wear that coat all the time, but even if you like certain predators, doesn't mean they will not eat you."

" What are you talking about, mom? Those beasts don't eat us."

" Yeah, they blow up in our faces," Antonio included.

" Antonio, you're not really helping," I said. "What I'm trying to say here, is that I know how to deal with them. Just let me be. Trust me on this."

My mom looked at me with a very serious face, questioning my expertise in this thing, given that she had never ever seen me communicate with green beasts before that.

" Fine," she ultimately said. "Go and do your thing. Just do not get yourself or anyone else hurt."

" I will not. Thank you, mother!" I said as I ran out the door, followed by Antonio.

We ran towards the other side of the hill and saw what the messenger had actually been talking about There were monsters everywhere, and they were headed towards the village.

" There are a lot of them," Antonio said. "What are you going to do?".

" Just watch me," I said. "Stay here."

I moved down the hill and snuck up on the beasts. Then I put my two fingers in my mouth and whistled as loudly and highly as I could, but not just like that ... with a particular pitch and tune to it! The green beasts recognized it and turned around. Slowly but certainly, they were walking towards me.

" Don't show them that you're terrified," I said to myself. "Don't reveal any indications of worry. It will be fine."

I whistled again. The beasts were very close now.

And that was the very moment I waved my arms in the air and jumped on one foot. I am certain that it looked absurd from a far distance, and Antonio was most likely making fun of me when he saw me do that, and yet I knew for sure that this would work. There is a certain way to interact with green beasts, and this was the approach I had actually read about.

After some more hopping, I stopped and said, "You will follow me! Follow me, now!". The monsters stopped moving towards me and patiently awaited my next move. I navigated my way through them and signified for them to come. What occurred next, was the most impressive thing any boy Antonio's age had ever seen. The green beasts were lining up and were following me into the opposite direction of the town. For miles and miles, they stayed in line. Antonio was following us at a range, and like an army commander, I marched far from our hometown and led the monsters to a far-off valley. 2 hours later, I ordered them to stop. I yelled that they should rest there, and they were scattered across the valley within minutes.

That's when I left them.

I climbed the hill and joined Antonio, who was looking at the valley and looking at me with big eyes. "Wow," he said. "I mean, I trusted you, but I didn't know you were able to do that."

" Pretty good, isn't it?" I said, feeling flattered.

" Yes. You know a lot about green beasts! It's awesome!".

" Thanks," I said, and I kissed him on the cheek.

" Uhm ... Carissa," he started. "Could you take off your hoody one more time and after that kiss me? I really want to see your beautiful red hair."

This lovely young guy knew the road to my heart. I removed the hoody and kissed him on the other cheek. After that, we returned to the town to tell everyone the wonderful news. This was the best day of my life.

THE END

Spying on the Neighbors

1: Missions

Stayla Village and Feron Ville do not like each other much. I've seen it numerous times. In fact, they hate each other. They can't stand each other. They constantly belittle each other and chatter till you tell them to change topics. Borders are tight, interaction is scarce, and most of the people from Feron Ville won't even come to our cozy town. What I appreciate is my own morals, the important things I believe in most. I believe in a certain degree of sincerity, in acceptable conduct, and generous acts of service to our fellow beings. I care about the courage to combat for what is right and the bravery of saying how it is. That last thing I mentioned isn't simple for a spy, though.

My name is Vincent, but my code name is Code-Fro, master of disguises. I took that code word to hide my true identity. You see, as a spy, you are under the stringent commitment to conceal things. And although I honor my commissioner and my place of origin, I will show you in this diary how I completely released those constraints in order to keep my integrity. I will tell you why I chose to throw all those guidelines away and found a new purpose.

The commissioner is my employer. He tells me what to do. It's that simple. However, his missions are always told to me in secret. I get an envelope, an email, a text, or a telephone call through a safe and secure line without anybody eavesdropping or learning about our conversation. Nevertheless, the funniest cases are when my manager, Commissioner Dallin, appears in a secret place. Of course, at first he scares me to death by turning up out of nowhere, but later on I always value the creativity of it. In the past, he has given me messages by putting his head above the water, diving out of a dumpster, or hiding in a wedding cake while licking the whipped cream off the top. You need to give this guy some credit for his efforts. No one expects it and it's amusing. Later I would discover his dark side though, but ... oh well ... more about that later.

" This discussion never occurred," is normally the ending line of my employer. He conceals everything he considers necessary.

In my backpack, I carry a list of items: A sword (I love that thing), a piece of string, crystals, and ... yes that was it. For a minute, I thought there was something else in there, but there isn't. This is my total list of products. Some of those items come in really handy when I am appointed to a mission. Other ones just remain in there for fun. Whenever I haven't used an item for a very long time, I put it in the back on the shelves in my closet. Utterly ineffective stuff doesn't belong in my bag.

Anyway, now that you know a little about me-- I mean, whatever else I tell you is just a bunch of gibberish you probably do not care about-- I will narrate, to the best of my ability, the intriguing situations that changed my perspective on the politics of our society. Things aren't always as they appear, and discovering the truth can be tough if you do not open your eyes and ears to find out about it.

So here we go, the story of how my mission turned into a tensed decision to turn my back on everything I was taught.

So there I was, minding my own business and walking through a narrow street with trees, bushes, and a line of several small homes.

" Psssst!" I heard behind me.

I turned around.

It was Commissioner Dallin.

" Code-Fro, I have an assignment for you."
Where was he hiding? I recognized his voice but could not find him anywhere.
" Over here, you imbecile. I'm over here," he said.
He was hiding in a plant, covered with dirt and flowers. It was tough to see him, and he deserved some definite bonus points for staying in there for so long (I could only imagine how long he had actually been there).
" Commissioner, how good to see you. Those flowers look great on you," I said while chuckling.
" Cut the BS. I have a supersecret objective. Are you ready to face one of the biggest difficulties you've ever dealt with?" he asked.
" You always say that, commissioner, and then it ends up it was just easy as pie."
" I know, but this time I mean it. This is tough and of the utmost importance. Here, read this."
He handed me a paper with some doodling on it. The back of the paper had a clear message.

Must take Cat Disc of 13 in the Feron Ville. Top secret. Don't tell anyone, not even your dog. Damage this piece of paper by burning it, ripping it, drowning it, putting it in an empty room and letting it decay where no one can find it, or simply letting a horse step on it. Just some tips ...

The commissioner was a little weird, I thought. Why would he elaborate on all the ways of how you could destroy the paper? It made no sense, but yeah, he never did.
" I like your tips, but do you realize that I do not have a pet dog?" I said.
" No. Next time I'll scratch that. Sorry. So tell me, are you prepared to steal the disc?"
" Of course, sir. Just tell me where and when."
" You will head to the Feron king's event of his spouse's birthday," commissioner Dallin said. "I already arranged the invite. I will also give you the coordinates of the disc, so you can find it and take it with you without being discovered. Report to me tomorrow at 17:00 hours."
" Yes, sir."
I walked away, wondering how he was going to get out of that plant and not stick out in the crowd, but he would find a way. He always did.

I arrived at the party that was being thrown in Feron Ville. The queen's birthday was a big day for the event.

" Good," I thought. "It helps me to stay undetected. No one is focusing their attention on the disc."

I was dressed up in fancy clothes. A black tuxedo, red bow tie, and a costly pair of shoes were my choice that night. Just like all the other people there, I followed the crowd up the outside stairs into the ballroom of the palace. Cameras were watching me, and I instantly spotted them, noticing the angle at which they were turned. There was a blind spot in each room, which could be convenient.

The ballroom was elaborately decorated with gold and mirrors, revealing fancy crimson red and royal blue patterns in the drapes and table cloths. A chandelier was hanging above the hall, with a hundred diamond crystals that reflected the incoming light, setting the sphere for the entering visitors.

Waltzing couples moved on the sound of old-fashioned, classical music. Beautiful gowns and ballroom gowns showed every color of the rainbow, and distinguished gentlemen acted more swank than ever to make a great impression on those they talked with. People interacted socially, drank, and chomped on the treats that were being given to guests. None of the elite inhabitants of this stunning city understood the fact that they were about to get robbed by me.

" What do you think about the new statues in the yard?" a woman asked.

" Lovely. simply wonderful," a man said.

" Who was the designer again?" another chic girl asked.

" The duke of Ravin," the man said.

" I heard it was just a little boy who had absolutely nothing to do with his life, got bored, and drew a funny figure to accompany his toys," I said, all of a sudden joining the discussion I overheard.

" And where would you hear such outrageous rubbish, young man?" the gentleman in the suit asked.

" I spoke to a little birdy," I said. "I'm sorry, sir. I was only joking. The designer must be a genius, I'm sure. Allow me to present myself. My name is Mr. Finley. Ladies ..."

I nodded at the 4 women surrounding the gentleman who just became a lot less popular.

" Well, you definitely show an unique way of joking around," the man said.

" Unlike yourself, I presume? I'm glad to see you are laughing so hard though, because I forget to laugh when I'm in the presence of such eloquent charm."

A few of the women were blushing. One of them got a fan and began fanning her face, secretly hiding behind the thing so she could glance above it, thinking it would help her fade into the background.

" Now, if only I could choose which of you pretty ladies to request for a dance ..." I said.

I saw the desire on their faces. One of them giggled and went back. Another's pupils got very big.

" Ah, I know," I continued. "I forgot I was being late. The king asked me to accompany his lovely partner and daughter to introduce the party and the birthday of his marriage partner. I'm already late. Excuse me, ladies, I."

I stopped briefly. I sniffled. I looked a little unusual, got out my handkerchief, and was about to blow my nose.

" Hold on a second, I need to ... Whoa! Whoops!" I said as I dropped my handkerchief on the floor.

" Oh, my ... I've never seen such awful manners," the gentleman said, looking the other way.

" Ladies ... sir. If you could please excuse me ..." I said.

" With satisfaction," The gentleman said, sticking his nose up in the air.

I left the uncomfortable circumstances and smiled. I didn't do anything without a strategy. I hadn't really dropped the handkerchief by accident. Before I went to them, I had observed several guests, following the guidelines in the information I had gotten from Commissioner Dallin. The big-headed gentleman in the suit who thought he was so high above everyone else, was actually carrying the access card to the room behind the throne room, the one in which the cat disc was hidden. If only the information were correct, it would help me get the disc in a heart beat, because all I was doing when I "inadvertently" dropped my tissue, was bend over and nab away the card from the gentleman's pocket in a fast, undetectable move. During my training as a spy, I had developed abilities like that, abilities that were excellent for those who want to pickpocket in an elegant ball like this one.

" What an odd boy," the man said, watching me walk off, not understanding I had just lost the important access card in his pocket.

Everything went according to plan.

Pleased with the way I dealt with the circumstances there, and particularly with the slick trick I used to take the access card, I left the ballroom and snuck behind the scenes into the little corridor behind the throne room. A high tech system showed that a code was needed to get in. I glanced around, making sure I wasn't being followed.
Nobody there.
The coast was clear.
Ready to go into the correct room to finish the objective.
I took the access key out of the left chest pocket in my blouse and inserted it into the alarm.
" Access granted," was all I heard.
I opened the heavy door and saw nothing. It was pitch black in the room. Where was the light switch? I put the access card back in my pocket and felt the surface area of the walls to find the light switch.
" Don't bother," a voice in the dark said. "The light switch is on the other side."
Who was that? I was surprised to hear another person in the room. I was almost desperate to find out who beat me to the punch, or who would know I would come here. I reached out to the other side and hit the light switch. The lights in the room turned on. On a big chair behind the desk sat a dubious figure with a brown hat and sunglasses. He leaned backward easily and didn't appear to care one bit about what was going on. Confidently, he left his dirty boots on the desk and smirked.
" Who are you?" I demanded. "And how did you know I would be here?"
" Oh, I see a lot more than the electronic cameras do," the guy said.
He got up and took off his sunglasses. Standing behind the desk, he continued his explanation.
" Looking for this, aren't you?" he asked, holding the right cat disc in his right hand.
" How did you ...? What is going on here?" I asked.
" That's precisely what I would like to know, which is why I broke in before you did. Unlike you, I am not from Stayla Village . Actually, I just live around the corner, two rocks away from this palace. Sorry, I didn't mean to confuse you, so I'll let you know what's going on here."
I still didn't trust this suspicious individual, but I was curious to hear what he had to say. So I stalled and listened patiently.
" I totally forgot to introduce myself. I have many names. I am a spy like you, but I work for Feron Ville. For now, you can call me Jerry. You might wonder why I am here, in this room, since I work for the other side. Well, let me tell you what I found. First off, do you have any idea what's on this disc?"
" No," I confessed. "I was just given the task to take it. That's all."
" They sure know how to conceal their sleaze," Jerry said in a cynical way. "I hope I can persuade you to see things from a different perspective. I mean, you most likely know just like everyone else that the people in Feron Ville and Stayla Village aren't actually fond of each other. But the truth may surprise you. Neither of these towns lack corruption. Tensions have been high for the past few decades, each of them declaring that the other one is a threat to their beautiful society. Both cities have been about to declare war a dozen times."

" Then why didn't they?" I asked.

" Well, the reason they wanted to declare war is to take each other's resources. You're most likely aware of the gold near the city here and the coal and gas near Stayla Village , aren't you?"

" Of course."

" Right. So there's your reason, but to the average resident, this is insufficient. They have to believe they are the heroes, that the others have a genuine reason to be conquered. And that, my fellow spy, is what they have been working on for several years."

" I'm beginning to get it," I said. "Why should I believe you?"

Jerry took his belt off and drew a gun from his pocket, after which he positioned it on the desk and put his hands up in the air.

" I'm here. You can just kill me now if you think I do not speak the truth. I know you have a sword in that bag, so go ahead."

" Okay," I said. "Even if I were to trust you, what do you want to do about it? Propaganda is everywhere. In Stayla Village , the plaques and posters are all over town, depicting Feron Ville as some evil town full of monsters. Not everyone is sure about the validity of the government's claims, but most people are starting to lean towards the war mindset."

" I've been wondering about that myself," Jerry said. "We have to create a strategy, you and me."

" So what's on the disc?"

" Oh yeah, the disc. I forgot to tell you. Are you prepared for this? Soldiers of Stayla Village actually blew up their own mine to make it look like there was a hazard. They made sure to leave enough evidence to show that Feron Ville soldiers did it, despite the fact that they had absolutely nothing to do with it. You know, Feron army pieces, flags, and small objects from this city ... to show that they had done it and sloppily left behind a few objects. This disc, though, contains secret videos from a bypassing civilian who put the entire attack on tape. When he was found, he ran for his life and handed the tape to the Feron king, who had one of his servants put the video on this disc."

Jerry put his belt back on and his gun in its holster.

" This disc could divulge the fact that Stayla Village soldiers blew up their own mine and tried to blame it on Feron Ville. Don't you see? Your commissioner is just trying to cover their tracks so they have a reason to begin a war!"

I thought for a moment. I saw the severity of the circumstances. After a second or 2, I said, "But if the Feron king shows this video to Feron Ville, they will feel upset as well! They will discover that Stayla Village is making an attempt to blame for something they didn't do."

" Exactly, and that's why none of these rulers can use this against the people of their cities. I just recently found out, but I saw you in the ballroom and I just knew you weren't from around here. That's why I just waited here after I got through security myself."

" Are you thinking what I am thinking?" I asked.

" I don't know. How can I know if I'm thinking what you're thinking if I don't know what you're actually thinking?" Jerry asked, returning the question.

" Well, I just thought we were thinking about the same thing," I said.

" How do you know if you don't even know what I'm thinking?" Jerry asked.

" Never mind," I answered. "This is going nowhere. So here is what I was thinking ... If I'm correct the hatred towards the Feron people is bigger in Stayla Village than the hatred towards the miners in Feron Ville."
" Exactly. So what?"
" So the one side is more likely to change their minds and become friendly and peaceful again is the king of Feron Ville, not the mayor or commissioner in Stayla Village ."
Jerry nodded. "I'm still following you," he said.
" We need to give the Feron king some kind of sign, a token of friendship. That way, it will set off a generous response in him, and the risks will be over."
" Maybe," Jerry said. "It's worth a shot. What do you have in mind?"

I did have something genius in mind. After leaving the ballroom and the celebration for a little while, I went home. Jerry promised to destroy the cat disc and accepted to see me the next day at 20:00 hours in the street beside the palace.

At home, I drew a map. I came up with a plan. I put everything on paper that I had learned about one of the most valuable products worldwide: Emerald rock. I knew they had it. They safeguarded a huge rock in the main town hall, surrounded by alarms and guards. It was so important that handing this over to the Feron king would help them ease up immediately.

If only the king would be generous enough to return something to Stayla Village , our plan would work. If not, the villagers here would claim that the Feron people would have taken it and it would activate a war anyway. It was a delicate circumstance, with psychological minds of dumb crowds all set to get angry over absolutely nothing. But if I didn't do anything, the war would eventually be set off anyway.

I prepared notes, looked at times, and determined the outside walls of the town hall. The next day, it would actually happen. I would steal one of their most valuable things, from my own home town.

When I got up, I took a walk. As I walked through the village streets, I noticed the posters in the streets, with words like, "Don't trust the Feron people," and "The differences between Feron civilians and rats: None." Some of them were more severe than others. This hatred was pure brain washing. I had been to Feron Ville various times, and none of this held true. It was all just a huge conspiracy to trigger a war and take their resources and their gold. But I was determined to stop this absurdity. Someone had to show them the truth.

I had changed sides. I had turned around. Often, it felt like I betrayed my own town. But I knew it was right. It was the only ethical thing to do. And it was going to occur that day.

5: The Alarm

I covered my face like a ninja. I wasn't going to show anybody my true identity, not when I was stealing something. It would be dreadful if anybody found out that it was me.
It was late. I had waited till dark. I put on my backpack and headed to the village hall. It was surrounded by bushes and trees in a lovely green garden. At first sight, none of those things seemed to be dangerous or potentially alarming, but I didn't trust it. I stepped closer, little by little, and after that, I saw it.
The rocks on the side weren't just rocks. I blew in the air. The breath from my mouth uncovered what the rocks were really for: Laser beams.
After looking in my backpack, I took out some crystal I had always kept with me. Carefully, I put the crystal between the laser beams. The alarm didn't go off. The crystal had some reflecting or bouncing effect on the lasers. It was perfect!
I held the crystal in the center and like an experienced thief, I very carefully stepped through the laser beams, ducking to avoid the upper beam and lifting my feet to get over the bottom one.
Fortunately, I was able to do all this without making a sound. I pulled the crystal out of the laser beam and continued to the front door. It only took me minutes to crack the code of the alarm. The villagers always had a fixation with the number 5, so codes like 555 or 345 were the only ones I tried. With a little device I had bought, I could put in as many codes as I liked, so that the alarm would not go off after my 2nd or third effort. After about 10 different combinations, I did it.
Gradually unlocking the door, I kept the lights off and snuck into the corridor.
No guards.
Good.
According to the map and the information I could get, the rock of Emerald stuff should be in the center of the structure. Stepping sideways with my back against the walls, I took my time. If anyone was in this structure, I would ensure I would not get caught.
After leaving a couple of rooms in there, I got in the designated room.
There it was.
It was gorgeous.
It had a black-greyish color and some green specks in it. Definitely, this looked like an incredibly important natural source.
The rock was secured, however. It was surrounded by a glass tank or container, and it would set off the alarm if raised from its pedestal.
No fear though. I had it all under control.

I reached in my bag again and pulled out the piece of string and the sword. I leaned over and observed the item for a minute or two.

" Okay, okay," I told myself. "I can do this. Just take it really slow."

I lifted the glass container.

Nothing happened.

" Nice," I said. "Now just the weight trigger."

I put the glass container on the floor. Then I connected the sword to the piece of string and held it in my left hand. I put the piece of string with the sword on it between the pointing finger and the thumb of my left hand.

With my right hand, I lifted up the rock emerald. With my left hand, I slowly let the sword drop onto the pedestal, replacing the weight of the rock. If my estimations were right, the sword would weigh roughly the same as the rock.

Gradually.

Gradually.

Got it! Yes! It was the same weight! I was so relieved!

I put the rock in my backpack and snuck out. This was fantastic! I did it! I got the Emerald rock! And I did it all by myself. This truly was among the hardest things I had ever done, but in the end, I succeeded. I just showed them that ...

Waaaaeeeeeeeeeaaaaeeeeee!

Oh no. What happened?

I looked down. So that was what set off the alarm! I totally ignored the laser beams in the garden. In my bliss, I had just walked out with the rock in my bag, taking pride in my accomplishments and letting my guard down. And this is what I got for it: Trouble ... and dozens of guards on the way to take me.

I got caught up in my emotions; I stressed. I stood there like a stupid stiff, frozen and baffled by the alarming circumstances I had just put myself in. I didn't know what to do or where to go.

" There he is!" I heard them shout.

I needed to get out of there. It was already far too late to sneak out, and now they wanted me! I ran as fast as I could, leapt over bushes and walls, turned around corners, knocked over some crates with market food that were left in front of the houses, and even got on a rooftop.

They nearly lost me. My dexterity had nearly beaten them. Jumping from roof to rooftop, I was, eventually, out of sight, at least of the fat, slow ones that chased me. One of the guards, nevertheless, kept going and didn't let me go.

Why did I need to be challenged with some athlete or sports champion?

I leapt again and rolled to break my fall. I ran up to a wall, got onto the edge, and pulled myself over it. I looked back, but he was still there, chasing me as if it were the last thing he did.

" Aha! That will be my escape route," I thought as I saw a chimney on the left. I avoided to the chimney, climbed up into it, and let myself drop.

Booof!

I landed on a cold, spiky log.

" Ouch!" I cried out.

As quickly as I could, I stood up and ran out the front door of the home I had gone into. No one had seen me. I vanished in an alley, never to be seen again by my pursuers. At home, I took the rock out. I went to my closet and grabbed some paper, ribbons, and a marker. I was creative. I embellished everything perfectly. The note on the wrapped gift I made read,

To the Feron king. From Stayla Village . We want you to have this. Consider it a token of our trust. We value everything you do and want to work together with you in the future.

I attached the note to the covered rock, finished it up with some smooth ornaments, and left my home. It took an hour before I reached the street where the palace of Feron Ville was. I looked around but saw nobody. Was it time yet? I was five minutes early, so maybe I just had to be more patient.
" Pssst," I heard all of a sudden.
I turned around. It was Jerry.
" Do you have the Emerald rock?" he asked.
" I do."
" Great! Hand it to me and I will lay it in the throne room. The king will be thrilled."
I handed him the rock and watched as he took a tricky side door into the Feron Palace. My job was done. Now all we needed to do was wait.

The next day, there was a huge event in the area. I slept in, since I was so worn out from all the stress and anxiety and stuff I had done the previous night.

The parade woke me up. There were trumpets, tubas, drums, and event dancers. Everyone was happy. I watched it out the window and saw how many people from Feron Ville were intermingling with the citizens of Stayla Village. The majority of people were smiling and enjoying the celebration.

Most people ...

When I saw Commissioner Dallin's face, I hid behind the curtains. I wasn't ready to face him yet. I thought for a minute and got prepared. I put on my shoes and my jacket as well; then I opened the front door and moved between the many people in the crowd towards the town square.

This is where it would all take place.

This was the town's big moment.

There was an actual performing stage set up. The mayor of Stayla Village and the Feron king were shaking hands. Smiling at each other, they exchanged unheard words that signified hope. The Feron king took the fabric off a cushion one of his servants was holding. Underneath it was an enormous pearl. It was pretty and shiny; it was worth a fortune. The mayor accepted it gladly and gratefully. Then he turned to the masses and beckoned us to be quiet.

" With this, we have decided to form a union between the 2 towns," he said. "Feron Ville and Stayla Village will work together as partners and exchange economic advantages to help each other grow more powerful and more affluent. This will be the crucial agreement in the history of our town. Long live the king!"

Everybody cheered. Peace was secured. The contract was officially signed, and the 2 rulers stepped down to shake hands with the people in the crowd to make a friendly, politically correct impression. It was a happy moment.

But not everybody was happy.

I felt someone tapping on my shoulder.

" I know it was you," Commissioner Dallin said when I turned around. "You took that Emerald rock. I don't know how you did it, I don't know how to prove it, but I feel in my bones that it was you. That sword on the pedestal was yours. I don't know anybody else who has one like it."

I raised my mouth to the side and smirked, closing my eyes midway and raising one eyebrow.

" Great job for figuring it out, genius," I said. "But before you exert yourself to find some type of evidence of my betrayal, I have to caution you that I have seen what's on the cat disc. Do you have any clue what it may do to your profession if I tell anyone what your soldiers did to that mine?"

" You would not dare," he said.

" Try me," I answered.

" Even if you would, how do I know you even have that disc? You never reported to me. Perhaps it got lost or stolen. I think you're bluffing."

" Am I?" I asked rhetorically.

He had nothing else to say. He enraged, but he didn't want to take the risk. Naturally, I was bluffing anyway. The disc was already gone. But who cares? He didn't know that.

THE END

Wolves among Us

Chapter 1: The Thing about Wolves

My name is Sylania. I like the brown color of my hair. It suits me, and because I like it so much, I let it grow long, having it extend all the way to my lower back. It's a lot of maintenance, but I enjoy combing and brushing it every morning, and looking in the mirror and feeling a little vain.

I love going outdoors. We are living on the border of a huge pine forest, and I typically retreat and allow myself to smell up the fresh air. Have you ever smelled fresh evergreen? It's the best thing in the entire world! I also love the wildlife: I think it's interesting to discover more about foxes, wolves, or bears. The predators captivate me the most; their consistent drive to chase after others or enhance their lifestyle by going out there and hunting down small animals, is interesting.

I do not go to school anymore. I am 23, which, in this town, is pretty old for a girl not to be married. You see, with the medieval practices we had, it was more regular to wed a lot younger. Why didn't I get married yet, you ask? Oh, just because I wanted the right one. In a town as little as this, you only have a restricted number of choices. After that, you either leave or stay single. And I remained single, living by myself, 3 streets away from my parents.

I have to admit that I turned down a number of guys who asked for my hand in marriage... alright, 3 ... I turned down three of them ... okay, four, five ... fine, I denied 6 of them. Guilty! (Imagine me raising my hand). Let's just say that one was a weirdo, the other was conceited, another thought he owned me, one was a fruit cake, and the others were just not my type. I was looking for somebody a bit more-- how do I say it?-- dependable? Handsome? Inspired? I don't know.

Anyway, I am getting ahead of myself. I will move along with my story. Then you will find how all these things relate to what truly happened in this little town.

It all started with that day I went to the forest. The snow had melted, and all that there was left, were some puddles and dripping branches. The pine odor had returned, and I loved it. I walked around for about a half hour, searching for seasonal fruits or berries, when I saw something on the ground.

" What was that?" I asked myself.

I moved closer and bent over. It was an animal skin or something. It was grey. I picked it up and looked at it. It looked like a wolf skin.

Unusual.

I put my hand in it and noticed it was pretty dry. It felt fluffy and soft on the outside and it looked stunning. I didn't know where it originated from, but I didn't care either. It was mine now. Happy with my newly found item, I walked around some more and returned home.

At home, I put the skin in front of the fireplace, just to let it dry a little more and make sure there would not be any mold or bad bacteria inside.

I looked at it again.

I loved it.

That night, I had a dream. I dreamed that I was a wolf myself. I was running along with the pack the villagers had seen in previous years. We were attacking and pillaging the town homes. I didn't feel guilty about it. I was just assisting the pack to endure the winter. Hey, they had to eat too, didn't they? So I felt a little linked to these beautiful animals in the first place.

Would it be fun to be a wolf? It made me wonder.

Little did I know about what would happen the next day ...

Chapter 2: My Boyfriend or Something

He was new in the area, so perhaps that's why a few other women got on him. New meat! Hahaaargh! No, just kidding, I am not that eager. But I did actually admit he was good-looking. In fact, I couldn't withstand staring at him sometimes. He spoke with people with self-confidence and made sure everybody felt good about themselves by complimenting them continuously.

He did the same with me; I think that was the reason I found him so lovely too. He didn't hold back on applauding others, and he appeared like a decent guy. He worked as a blacksmith, a profession that had been overlooked for a while in this town, so there was a lot to do for him. He was 29, so a little older, and I was going to discover more about this strange man who was practically too good to be true. I put on my new wolf skin and left my house.

" Zelda, what are you doing here?" I asked one of my friends when I saw her walking into the same direction as I was.

" I could ask you the same thing," she said.

" Nowhere in particular," I lied.

" Well," she said, "then you won't mind if I go see the new guy in the area."

" There is a new guy in town?" I asked sheepishly.

" Oh, come on. Do not tell me you haven't heard of him yet. He's got muscles, because he is a blacksmith. At least, that's what I heard. And they say he is quite the looker."

" How nice, huh? You're still single too, aren't you? Maybe I will just join you and find out what he's like."

She didn't like that idea; I could tell. It meant competitors, but she didn't want me to see right through her either, so she pretended to not really mind whether I would come along or not. "Fine, do what you want," she said.

It was an uncomfortable moment, but we didn't have to walk far to reach the blacksmith's shop. When we got here, we saw how open everything was and how well the new guy had already been organizing everything.

" Hi," Zelda and I said.

" Hello there, girls. To what do I owe the privilege of your company?" he asked.

" We were just visiting to welcome you to your new home town," I said. "How are you liking it here so far?"

" It's not bad. I have seen many people visit this morning, and I am attempting to remember everyone's names. How about yourself?"

" Oh, we love it here," Zelda said. "Especially now that you're here."

She was moving way too fast on this guy. But he seemed to think it was funny. He smiled and asked me the same question again.

" It's a small town," I said. "But if you're creative, you can find things to do. And after that, there is always the forest. It's lovely over there. By the way, my name is Sylania, and this is my buddy Zelda."

" Lupo," the guy said. "My name is Lupo."

" That sounds great," I admitted. "It's like a wolf. How did you get that name?"

" There were lots of wolves in the area, and one day my dad told me that the one thing that makes the leader stand apart from the rest, is his intelligence."

" Hahaha!" Zelda chuckled. It actually wasn't that amusing, but oh well.

" Well, see you later, Lupo," I said. "I live in the greenish brown house on the other side of town. Be sure to come by sometime."

Zelda remained a bit longer. I liked the guy, but I didn't want to be self-important, if you know what I mean. I let him know where he could find me, and I swung by more often in the weeks after that.

In the 3rd week after he arrived, we got a lot closer to each other. We just talked and talked practically every day, and our friendship became more powerful as time elapsed.

I still remember the day he first kissed me. It was a spring day; it was hot outside, but there was a great breeze. We had discussed the people in the village, his blacksmith profession, some of his relatives, and the advantages and disadvantages about residing in a tiny town. He asked me about the wolf skin.

" Oh, that," I said. "I just found it in the forest. I do not know why. Some hunter must have left it there or something."

" It looks terrific on you," he said. "It's like ... it's totally you, you know?"

I blushed. "Thanks," I said. "Do you like wolves?"

He laughed. "Who likes wolves?" he asked. "They just assault the villagers and take your stuff."

" I don't know," I said. "They have something magic to them, however, with all that fur and their eager senses."

" Well, if you put it that way, then yes. I love wolves. I love the way they look, but I wouldn't want to come close to them. I knew a werewolf in my home town. That was quite the story. Don't get too close. Nevertheless, you are somebody I would love to come near to."

He pulled me towards him, and I let him. It all happened so quickly, but I was prepared. I was succumbing to this captivating guy, Lupo. He had something weird about him, as if he had not told me everything about his previous years yet. I found it scary yet exciting. He leaned over and came closer. Then I took the effort and kissed him.

From that moment, I knew I didn't want to wait any longer for another one to come along. I was ready to marry this guy, although it was still early. So of course, I didn't tell him that, but I secretly kept it in the back of my mind. After all, he was the guy; he was supposed to ask me to wed him. But I knew that I would say "yes" when the time would come. He took his time though. He didn't want to rush into anything, and I was quite happy with that.

From that time forth, we went to the forest more often and ate at my family's home. We dated often, despite the minimal amount of things to do in town. We ran in the hills, got some flowers, swam in lakes, and climbed up in trees. Everything nature had to offer, was at our finger tips. All spring and summer long, we had the best time of our lives. But then the winter season came ...

Things would become a little scarier around here ...

It was full moon. The wind was cold as ice. Snow had appeared again, and tracks were rapidly covered up by the falling snow. The weather was awful; the air was thin, and each villager could see his or her breath forming a fluffy cloud in front of them any place they went. The white snow contrasted the thick, black sky, reversing the brightness in the summer and painting a typical scene for a dreadful event to occur.

Outside, I met Lupo, who looked a little worried.

" What's wrong?" I asked.

" Business was bad this week," he said. "One of the villagers had me work on a shovel for three days but refuses to pay up. He says I didn't do a sufficient job, but I know that there is no other way to fix it."

" Who was it?"

" I think his name was Sander. Do you know him?"

" Yes, I do. He's always been a jerk. I do not know what the deal is, but he is never good to people. Don't take it personal in any way."

" I'm not. I wished I wouldn't have spent all that time on this specific item when I could have been doing other things."

I chuckled a little. "What other things are you working on?" I asked.

" I've been making some swords and shields ... collector's items for the wealthy. I think it will be an industry if I go abroad and sell them in the markets. At home, we were always hearing about the huge demand for those things."

" You and your aspirations," I said. "I love it. Have you always worked so hard?"

" Of course. It's part of life. Besides, it's not just for the money. If you work hard, you will find yourself becoming a better person. That's what my father taught me. Do you think that's real?"

" If he was referring to you, then yes," I said.

Then he kissed me and bid me farewell, saying that he still had a lot of work to do.

" Don't you want to snuggle up together in front of the fireplace?" I asked.

" No, thank you. Sorry, but not this time. I am very hectic. If I do not work this night, I will not have enough to eat for the next few days."

I felt for Lupo. He didn't deserve this treatment. I went home, a little sad.

Later on that evening, I was inside my hut. Since it was freezing outside, I had gathered all the wood I could find, with the help of my boyfriend. A big heap of logs was stacked against the sidewall of my cabin, and to make it even warmer, I had put the wolf skin on my body. The fireplace was warm, but on the front, so I ensured the wolf skin covered my back. There I was, staring at the flames, seated on a rug and wondering what the future would bring. I got drowsy, and it didn't take long before I was sound asleep, leaned against the wall, with the wolf skin covering my eyes.

I do not know for how long I was out, but I do know that I got up with a jolt because of a sound. The cabin walls in the village homes do not allow the villagers to have a ton of privacy. I've heard dogs bark, babies cry, men snore, and other interrupting noises I could not quite put my finger on.

A few times, I was sure the couple next door was having sex. Either that or the lady was yelling for some other reason, but with the consistency of the sounds, I could not help but believe that it was that: They were doing it. I guess it made being single even harder, since those sounds make you think about it, although I don't condemn my next-door neighbors for doing it. Hey, if they are happy and they are married, and they want to reinforce their relationship that way, then that is fine with me. It just felt a little uncomfortable when I heard them do it. It was not something I wanted to know a lot about, although I imagined, just for a short moment, and only one time, that it was me making the sounds and Lycus doing it in there with me. Anyhow, enough about that. This is about something totally different.

This time, the noise differed from something I had ever heard before.

" Eeeeeeeeeh!" one of the women squealed.

I ran outside as quickly as I could. I could feel the stress. The whole village was running backward and forward in the snow, attempting to figure out what the panic was all about. I saw my parents and some other familiar faces.

" What's going on?" I asked.

" Someone has been robbed," a man answered. "All his storage food is missing. We are coming together for a grand council."

I knew the council would not be very grand, since the town was small anyway, but I knew what they meant. It was only an hour later, late at night, that they put together the whole town, with the exception of mothers staying with their small children, to be gathered into the main village hall.

I was curious what was going to happen, because I knew absolutely nothing about it, except for what that guy had told me.

I entered the building and saw the fifty people who had the time to make it that night. Among them was my partner, Lupo. I said "hi" and asked him if he would not mind me sitting next to him. He nodded and I sat next to my sweetheart, after which I leaned my head on his shoulder.

" I'm worn out," I said while I yawned.

" Me too. Sssshhhh ... they're starting."

And the conference started.

" Ladies and gentlemen," the chief villager, whose name was Corian, began, "we are here this evening because a gross crime has been done. And as a united people, we need to figure out who did it and have him or her face the consequences. Will the victim please arise?"

Sander stood. "I have been robbed," he said. "I do not know who it is, but I saw him."

" Could you please explain yourself?" the chief villager asked. "How is it that you saw the perpetrator but didn't know him?"

" Because he was a wolf," Sander said.

Everybody marveled and was in shock. Some of them held their breath, others got huge eyes and looked at Sander in fear.

" A wolf?" Corian asked. "How do you expect a wolf to steal, Sander? Wolves don't even know where to search for your things."

" I don't believe it was a real wolf," Sander said. "It was a monster. I have never seen one like it before. It had green eyes, black fur, and it was at least 3 times bigger than I am."

" Sounds like a big beast," Corian agreed.

" Yes, and before it left the house, it said something to me. I couldn't understand it well, since it more or less sounded like a callous animal, but I think it was something like, 'Next time, pay up.'"

" Interesting. What do you suggest we do about it?" Corian asked.

" I don't know," Sander said. "I tried to follow the footprints, but they got all blended with the other villagers' footprints and some of them disappeared in the snow. Besides, after a while, they weren't even there anymore, having become human footprints going into all different directions."

" Sounds worthless then. But let's return to what the wolf was saying. What do you think it was referring to when it said, 'Next time pay up?'"

" I haven't paid a few people for their services. It could be one of them."

" Ridiculous," one of the villagers screamed as he stood up. "What are you accusing me of? You've known me for several years. Even if you happened to get robbed after overlooking to pay me, does not mean I am a monster."

" Calm down," Corian said. "We have not implicated you of anything yet. But since you're so defensive about it, would you care to discuss what Sander still owes you?"

" He owes me five pieces of gold. That's what."

Corian turned to Sander and asked him for an explanation.

" I'm sorry," Sander admitted. "I will pay you, first thing in the morning."

" Who else are you still indebted to?" Corian asked.

" That kid!" he unexpectedly yelled. "That guy, Lupo! He is new in town. How convenient to have a wolfman just after he appeared. I owed him money for a tool he repaired. He must be the werewolf."

" How dare you?" I said as I stood up. "Just because you do not know anything about him, does not mean you can implicate him of being a beast."

" He has motive," Sander said. "So how do you know your little partner over there isn't a huge werewolf? You don't."

" Lupo," Corian said. "What do you want to say in your defense?"

" I think that whoever took it, probably stashed it away somewhere. You're welcome to search my house. I do not have your food."
" Good response, Lupo. Let's go take a look at your place after the conference."
" Fine," he said.

They discovered absolutely nothing, and I was feeling better. I didn't want my handsome Lupo getting locked up for being a werewolf. That would be ludicrous. I just knew he would never do something like that, although people who become wolves do things they would otherwise never do.

It made me wonder ... what if the wolfman was real? Sander wasn't making it up, was he? But then, who could have taken the food? We had never had a werewolf in the area before. This was something entirely new, which was why it frightened the villagers even more. I had become aware of wolfmen in other towns, far-off rumors of foreign lands and such. They said they only appear when it's full moon. So during the next moon cycle, I would be waiting to snatch this wolf.

A month later, we were still dating, Lupo and I, and the weather had remained the same, along with the secret of who could have been the werewolf. But the full moon was nearly there, and all the villagers were nervous.

" What do you think will happen?" I asked Lupo.

" I do not know, but if the werewolf strikes again, I will be waiting," he said.

" It will be tonight. Can you keep me company tonight?"

" Of course," he said. "I will protect you."

I gave him a hug.

That night, I was a little nervous, but I knew I would be safe in his arms. We met up at my place, preparing the same relaxing fireplace for a night of falling asleep in each other's arms. I was eagerly anticipating it, but when he came inside, I quickly saw how worn out he was from getting up early and working throughout the day.

We only talked for a few minutes, after which he fell asleep on the rug on the floor. I lay beside him and conked out after a significant amount of time as well, covering myself up with the wolf skin.

After a few hours, I awakened. I opened my eyes and found that my partner had left me. What was going on here? I thought he would sleep next to me? This didn't make any sense. Was he the werewolf? No. Not possible. He was so sweet and kind and ...

I stood and looked around me. Apparently, he had left my cabin. I put out the fire and walked out the door. Then I saw a stain on my gown. Yuck, was that tomato sauce? Or was it blood? I couldn't see the difference, so I licked it. Yep, it was tomato sauce. Weird.

It was dark, but the snow reflected the pale moonlight, and I could see as far as in the daytime. I knew it most likely wasn't the wisest thing to do under the full moon, since the villagers still hadn't caught the werewolf, but I snuck through town to Lupo' house.

There he was ... was that Lupo? Or was that somebody else? Hey, was he attempting to get into his backdoor?

" You! Stop it right there!" I shouted.

He looked at me and started running. I could not see his face. It looked like a shade, a figure that quickly ran in despair. It had to be the wolf, although it didn't look like a wolf from that distance. Perhaps it was the one who had turned into a werewolf before.

There was only one way to know for sure: Run after him!

I ran towards Lupo' home and yelled, "Lupo!"

No one home, not even when I went inside for a few seconds.
Odd. So maybe it was Lupo after all. In either case, I continued pursuing the suspicious shade. I was slowly gaining territory on him. I thought he probably didn't think I was pursuing him anymore, because I saw him standing in the forest behind a tree.
I ran and ran ... and ...
THUD!
I ran into the fleeing fugitive.

" Lupo?" I asked.

" What are you doing here?"

" I got up and noticed that you were gone, so I went through every street looking for you. Ultimately, I looked at my home, but you weren't there. Then you screamed, but I thought you were another person, so I ran into the forest. Does that make sense?"

" Not at all. Why are you saying I was gone? I was at my place the whole time until I began looking for you."

" Uhm ... no, you weren't. I woke up and you were gone. That's precisely how it happened. By the way, did you see all that food that was accumulated in my home? Where did it come from, really?"

" I have no idea," I said. "Yes, I saw it. But hold on a minute, when I awakened, you were gone."

" What? This is getting a lot stranger by the minute. How come we missed each other? One of us left first."

" Well, it sure wasn't me," I said, being completely convinced of my innocence.

Then he looked at my dress. "Sylania," he started, "is that from the tomato sauce in my house? Why would there be tomato sauce on your dress?"

I looked down as if I had not seen it before. "I do not know," I said with huge eyes while I shrugged.

" No," he said after a while, going back and covering his mouth. "It can't be ..." He looked scared.

" What are you saying, Lupo?"

" Y-you," he said. "You are the werewolf?"

" What? Don't be crazy. How could I be the werewolf?"

As I said it, it all came back to me. I looked at the wolf skin I had picked up. I felt the remarkable power streaming through it. And even though I wasn't a wolf anymore, I could still feel it, seeing that it was still full moon and all. I took the skin off and looked at it. As quickly as I looked at the eyes of the wolf's head, an abrupt rush of memories went through my mind.

I recalled everything ... the night I turned into a wolf to steal Sander' food and give it to Lupo, the place I hid it from the town's people; and the moment a few hours ago, recently, that I snuck out as a wolf, leaving him there to sleep on the carpet without him seeing me, and taking the stash to his home. I looked at the tomato sauce on my dress and remembered how I spilled the sauce on me when I was carrying the food to Lupo' storeroom.

" Wait," I said. "I can explain. I was only trying to help; don't you see? I didn't even remember doing all that up until now. You have to believe me."

" I do not know what to believe anymore," he said, after which he looked me in the eyes and ran away.

I watched him being afraid of me, rushing back to his safe home, away from me. Our trust was gone. He believed that I was the monster they were looking for, and when I thought of it, he was even right. I was the werewolf. I had been the wolf all that time, and I had not even realized it, because each time, after a night of ransacking and stealing, I had awakened on my comfortable rug in front of the fireplace, with my clothing back on, for some mystical reason.

I walked back and hoped he wouldn't tell the other villagers. My subconscious mind had tried to help him, since he wasn't earning enough. I looked at the town. Everybody was still asleep. I didn't think he warned anybody else, but I was hurt. I was frightened that I was capable of robbing another person in this monstrous form. What was I going to do?

I didn't see Lupo for another week. He stayed away from me, that was for sure. I even walked by his store a few times, but he would always just look at me and after that, he would keep banging on a piece of steel or something.

I didn't blame him, in one way or another, but I was dissatisfied, to say the least, that our relationship had taken a step backwards like this. I felt lonesome and unhappy.

The next day, however, someone came to me, someone I had never seen in the area before. He approached me with his spouse and immediately introduced himself.

" Are you Sylania?" he asked.

" That depends on who is asking," I said.

" I am Lupo' father and this is his mother. We heard a ton of good news about you."

" Oh yeah?"

Lupo' father continued, "We heard how you tried to help our son with his food storage. It was very brave of you to do it that way, but what I am wondering, is ... can I have that wolf skin back that I lost in the forest?"

My mouth fell open. Lupo' dad was the one who lost this mysterious wolf skin? Was his father a werewolf? Wow. I didn't expect that.

" Uhm ... obviously," I said. "I liked it. It kept me warm all winter. And there are a ton of other things you can do with it too."

" I know," the dad said. "But before this entire village starts implicating you of the same things as they accused me of, back in my home town, how about you just hand it over? That way, you can stay out of trouble and I will have what was rightfully mine."

" And don't stress over the skin, dear," Lupo' mother added. "We will give you another one with uhm ... less eccentric capabilities."

" Sounds like a bargain to me," I said.

I returned home to get it and saw Lupo was standing there.

" I just met your parents," I said.

" I know," he answered. "They wanted the wolf skin back, didn't they?"

" Yes, I didn't know it belonged to your dad."

" Well, in either case, you can give them this one," he said, handing me the magical wolf skin I had found. "And this one is for you," he said as he gave me another wolf skin.

" Thanks," I said.

" Oh, Sylania," he said, stopping me from turning around, "there is something inside the new wolf skin I just gave to you."

" Okay. I'll look at it some other time."

" C-could you look at it now?" he asked shyly.

I don't know what this guy was up to, but he sparked my interest. I consented to humor him and reached inside the wolf skin's fur. It was a thing, cold and most likely made of metal. I pulled it out and looked at it.

" What is this?" I asked, but when I looked at him, I saw him kneeling down on one knee. He grabbed my hand and proposed.

And guess what ... I said YES!!!

Nobody ever bothered looking for the werewolf again, because during the next few moons, no one spotted it. It would be pointless anyway, since the wolf skin I now had, wasn't magical or unique in any sense.

Well, actually, it was special in the sense that it was the place I found my engagement ring. That was unique enough to me. I never got rid of it. And each winter season, we were in front of the fireplace and snuggled up under the warm wolf skin Lupo had given me.

THE END

Disappearances

Chapter 1: That Thing

Bellagio still recalls the day it was built. The "Shining Star" monument depicts a man and a woman in warrior clothes holding a sword in one hand at the bottom and raising their left hands in the air promoting a star. The man and woman look young and innocent, but have a determined expression on their faces. They are the sign of the country's youth, the future generation.

Its message is that the youth from today will be tomorrow's leaders, and that taking care of them, is one of the adults' biggest responsibilities. It's about 50 feet high. The statue is paved with gold.

The elegance of the statue surpasses all competing tourist sights and draws in travelers from all over the world. Countless everyday photographers come to observe the magnificence and symbolism of this monument, which is put in the center of the huge metropolis.

Bellagio enjoys the statue. His goals to get married and have kids at some point are still in the back of his mind. He sighs as he looks up and remembers his own heroic days in the army, about five years ago, when he was fighting off invading enemies in the forest and securing the offspring of others who relied on the soldiers' real heroism.

" Those were the real good old days," he says. And although those minutes were filled with death and destruction, he also recognizes the daring wars have made him stronger.

" Well, I better go home," he says after finishing his lunch on a bench. He glances at the statue one more time and betakes himself to his place.

It has been a lazy day; one of those odds and ends days that require somebody to repair this, make a telephone call there, or sign some dull documentation. Bellagio works for the city's main detective office, a place so big that they need 5 floors with coworkers and managers to fill the place. He is just one of many, and he never got a complicated task before.

Most of the cases he has solved, involved finding a missing cat, intervene in marital relationship disagreements, and an actual crime committed by a non-threatening thief. He doesn't mind, though. He is pleased with his life. Why would he try to do more? He has done this for several years now and he is good at it. Too bad his superiors do not acknowledge that, but Bellagio is confident that they will give him some larger cases to solve sooner or later.

He leans back in his comfy chair. It does not appear like anything major is about to happen anyway. Reports of criminal offenses have decreased, and the city has been fairly peaceful recently.

" The more reason to sleep better," Bellagio says before he decides to close his eyes. Then he goes to sleep on his chair after drinking from a huge cup of hot chocolate.

The next morning, when Bellagio comes to the detective workplace, everything is in commotion. Employers are running from one end of the room to the other, documentation is all over the floor, and it seems like half of the people there are on the phone.

" What is going on here?" Bellagio asks one of his friends, whose name is Casper.

" You mean to say that you have not even heard it?" Casper asks.

" No. That's why I am asking."

" The monument is down, man. It's gone, and nobody has the smallest idea what happened to it, nor when it happened. The whole department here is preoccupied with it. They need answers before the population goes crazy."

" And when will that be?" Bellagio asks.

" I do not know, but you know how it is. Whenever some disaster happens, people get scared, and when they worry, turmoil isn't too far away anymore. We've got to do something."

Then Bellagio's manager comes at him. "Bellagio," he says. "Why are you late? Do you have any idea what sort of a mess we are in?"

" Casper just told me," Bellagio says.

" Well, aren't you fortunate to have a friend. Now, get to your computer and begin doing some research to help us out. We are desperate."

" Excuse me, Sir," Bellagio says, "but would not the best way to do research be at the spot where it happened? What are we going to find here? It certainly didn't occur at the office."

" Oh, so you think you're smarter than me, don't you? Well, in that case, I've got an idea."

Bellagio is shocked when he hears his employer say the following, "Ladies and gentlemen, can I have your attention, please? From now on, Bellagio is the lead investigator for this case! He will be in charge! Thank you! Carry on."

" What? What are you doing?" Bellagio asks. "I've never solved a case this big."

" Then here is your chance to prove your worth," his employer says. "If you fail, I will fire you. So you better make it a success."

" Great," Bellagio says sardonically while rubbing his head and watching him leave. "From absolutely no responsibility to leading the entire department."

As quickly as he looks the other way, five people stand in front of him.

" Uhm ... hi," Bellagio says. "What can I help you with?"

" Bellagio, where should I put these documents?" one of them asks.

" Do you want me to call the mayor again and request for a public declaration?" a woman asks.

" Can you help me format this file I am dealing with?"

" Which telephone number should I refer the journalists to?"

" What things have we found so far, and am I at liberty to reveal them?"

It ends up being too much. Bellagio feels overwhelmed. He isn't sure how to assist all these people, so he says, "That's it! Line up. I am going to answer your questions one by one. You first. Let's go."

After about an hour of responding to questions and organizing the department, Bellagio is finally finished.

" That was a huge stack of work, wasn't it?" Casper asks.

" Yes, it was. I am prepared to get out of here. How about you?"

" Definitely," Casper says. "Let's get some sandwiches for lunch."

The duo leaves the office building and heads to the closest lunchroom. Once they are inside, they order a large pepperoni sandwich and a curry chicken sandwich. They take a seat and wait for the waiter to bring it over. Bellagio isn't particularly keen on the hard, wood chairs, but he keeps himself from complaining and sits down to listen to Casper.

" We need to get some hints," Casper says.

" I agree. I don't think the office is the best place to find anything."

" Right. So after lunch, shall we check out the monument scene?"

" You got it."

They finish their sandwiches-- Bellagio a lot faster than his friend-- and go to the area of the monument that has just disappeared that night.

" Wow," Bellagio says when they show up. "I didn't think it was possible."

They look at the empty square and stare at the spot where they saw a 500+ feet statue the previous day.

" Unbelievable," Casper says. "Nothing is left."

" Something must be there," Bellagio claims. "There is never a criminal activity without evidence."

" Still, how can you make a whole monument that huge disappear in one night?"

" Well, let's go over the possibilities," Bellagio says. "There is knocking it over and transporting it with the help of a semi-truck."

" Nearly impossible, I would say."

" Correct, so maybe a helicopter."

" Too heavy."

" Also correct. Then there is the possibility of blowing up the ground below it and having it drop into the sewage system ..."

" ... which didn't occur, because there is no hole in the ground."

" And that brings us to ..."

" Absolutely nothing."

Bellagio agrees. They've got nothing at all. But he still wants to look around. He walks backward and forward and puts his magnifying glass on the ground. Policemen are standing in the back, talking away and taking a break. Bellagio looks at the sky.

" Still ..." he mumbles, "we've overlooked one last possibility."

" Which is?" Casper asks.

" That the thief utilized magical items."

" Oh, come on, Bellagio. You know there is no such thing as a magical item."

Bellagio looks stunned. "I have combatted magic monsters in the borderlands. Do not tell me you don't believe in that. The world is mysterious. There has been proof of fire items, magical potions, and ultimate artifacts of power. Those are all sensible testaments from reputable people."

" I guess you're right, but what type of thing are you thinking about?"

" No idea, Casper. I have no idea. I think we need to question people and discover more about this unexpected secret."

" Let's begin knocking on some doors there," Casper suggests.

Bellagio and Casper start in the closest streets to the monuments. They knock on lots of doors, but they can't get much important information from the city people.

" One day it was there, and after that it wasn't," a big man says.

" We were in bed. How should we know?" two little girls ask.

" Yeah, I've seen it," a man who smells like alcohol claims. "It was a magic moment, you know. The statue has gone to heaven. The symbol of justice and mercy, the ultimate beacon of truth for the nation. I told them it would take place. As soon as the city would become wicked, the statue would disappear. But did they listen? Nooooo. They said I was insane, but I haven't slept for 3 days now and I last ate two days ago. Does that sound crazy to you? Ha-ha-ha-ha!"

Another door they knock on, has a huge, loud pet dog behind it. "What do you want?!" the owner shouts.

" We would just like to know if you've seen anything happen to the statue!" Casper screams back.

" Why? What happened to it?!"

" Never mind."

Another home is inhabited by an old woman. "You boys shouldn't bother tranquil civilians in this community. So shame on you," she says. "Look at me, for instance. When I was young, we didn't have telephones or computers. All you youths are spoiled. I needed to walk to school for 12 miles every day. I didn't have any shoes, so I made a pair of wood shoes with my bare hands, only to make 2 cents daily after milking the cows and doing 5 hours of homework when I came home. You never heard of text messaging or innovation back then. That's when people actually talked to each other."

" Well, that's uhm... very good," Bellagio says. "But do you know anything about the disappearance of the statue?"

" No," the old woman replies. "In fact, it was about time that ugly thing was gone. Do you know the number of times that glossy silver shone in my eyes? One time, I was walking on the street, and the reflection by the statue was ..."

" Good afternoon, Madam," Casper says, disrupting her and walking away.

They both walk into another street. The two investigators look disappointed. What are they going to do next?

Then Bellagio's phone is ringing in his pocket. He takes it out of his pocket and answers it.

" I think we found something," he hears one of the colleagues from the workplace say.

" I'll be there as fast as I can," Bellagio says. He hangs up and says, "Come on, Casper. Let's get to the bottom of this. Back to the workplace."

When they reach the office, they receive a report from a witness.

" This is Pablo," the coworker says. "He says he saw something last night."

" Speak up, so we can all learn what is taking place," Bellagio says.

They take a seat and Pablo starts, "I saw somebody walk towards it. I was just coming back from my nightshift at the hospital when it happened. I don't live too far from the statue, and I always take a little detour to see how well it's lit up. But this time, I observed a shady figure."

Bellagio and Casper laughed. "What precisely does a 'shady figure' appear like, Pablo?" they ask.

" Well, he looked up to no good and he had a black with yellow hat. Extremely ugly," Pablo responses.

" That does not mean anything," Bellagio says. "But please continue. What happened after that?"

" He stood in front of the monument and got something out of his pocket. It was a shiny thing, but I could not put my finger on what it was. Then he threw it at the statue and the statue disappeared."

" What?" Bellagio asks. "It just vanished, that easily? That does not make any sense."

" I know it doesn't," Pablo says. "But that's what I saw. I swear. After the statue had disappeared, the guy with the hat walked towards the empty area and picked up the glossy object, after which he put it back into his pocket. I was upset. I ran towards him, but before I knew it, he had already jumped into a car that pulled over and had the driver take him out of sight. It all happened so quick. There was nothing I could do."

" Okay. Thank you for the pointers. Would there be anything else that we should know about?" Bellagio asks.

" No, that was it. That was all."

" Thanks. We will continue this investigation with the new information. You can go home."

Chapter 4: The Crazy Pearl

" What did you get out of Pablo's testimony?" Bellagio asks.

" What do you mean? Exactly what you did, right?" Casper says.

" I guess you didn't get it," Bellagio says. "The black and yellow hat is only being used by people who live in Darcy County. The one who made the monument vanish is clearly from that area. And the glossy item that makes things disappear ... any idea what that could be?"

" Like I said, Bellagio," Casper begins, "I don't know much about those magic things. It could be anything, for all I know. But if you have any clue of what it might be, then please share your knowledge with me."

" It's a certain pearl," Bellagio says. "They are very uncommon, but when you toss them against an item, it makes that object teleport."

" To where?"

" Anywhere you're thinking of at the time you do it," Bellagio says. "It's a truly amazing item."

" What are you saying we should do?" Casper asks.

" We are going to Darcy County. I bet we will find the solution there."

No sooner said than done, the two detectives go on a trip to the distant land. They drive for about 7 hours southward and reach their destination. When they show up, the air feels thick. Darcy County is a tropical place with beaches and hotels on the coasts but a less outstanding history and government budget.

Bellagio immediately sees the difference. The population looks not as rich and they look desperate to make a quick buck. When he goes out of the car, 3 people come towards them to show them his new hotel or guide them through the city. Bellagio and Casper nicely decline unneeded services and set out on a journey to the city center of the capital.

What they see there, surprises them both.

" Oh, wow," Casper says.

" So that was it then," Bellagio agrees. "Casper, I think we might have found our motive."

The 2 investigators watch in wonder as a huge, red cloth gets pulled from a statue in the middle of the city square. The statue portrays a swirly dragon with 4 legs, lots of scales, hollow eyes, and a mouth with sharp teeth. Its disposition looks threatening and strong; the specific image the population is trying to sketch. The message they want to communicate is encrypted at the bottom of the monument: The Strong Rule.

Casper shivers. "Why would any person produce a statue like that?" he asks.

" The question is: Why would any person erect a statue at the same time that ours got taken?" Bellagio says.

They listen to the clapping of thousands of people who show their respect to the statue, which is almost as big as the taken youth statue from Bellagio's home town. The crowd is going wild when a ribbon gets cut and the mayor announces the dawning of a new period for this city, prosperity and abundance. He highlights the opening of new dining establishments, hotels, and sights in the city, all beginning with this new dragon statue.

" Hooray!" the residents cheer.

Bellagio and Casper watch the event, the band, and the dancers that add to the happy happening. It is obvious that some big financier in this enhanced tourist hub wishes to beat the competition, and has taken a first step by removing the "Shining Star" monument. Bellagio and Casper have already come to that conclusion.

" There!" Casper unexpectedly says, as he points to a man with a black hat and yellow ribbon on it.

" Well, he has the hat," Bellagio admits, "but so does that guy." He points to another man in the opposite direction. "And that woman," he says when he points at another person.

" Okay, alright. I just thought it could be the perpetrator. We need to find him, Bellagio, and take that dangerous pearl away from him."

" I think so too. Let's go to one of these hotels, since they're new and look nice anyway, and find out a way to uncover the truth."

Bellagio takes some pictures of the entire happening, and after a few minutes, they leave the city square and check in at one of the hotels' lobbies. They get the key to the room, take the elevator to the upper floor, and walk into their hotel room.

" Aaaah, this is the life," Casper says as he falls down on one of the beds.

" Get up," Bellagio says. "We have work to do. We need to investigate this case."

" Fine. Show me what you have."

" Well, these are the photos of the square. I also got a map from one of the organizers that shows us where the hotels and restaurants are going to be. And over here," he says as he points at a place on the map, "there will be night clubs and minibars. It's all set up so it can become a significant travel destination."

" But why is the statue so important?" Casper asks.

" Look at these names," Bellagio says.

Casper looks. All the names belong to a dragon. The monument is the central theme in the entire city. "Dragon Hotel, The Dragon Club, Dragon Moon Plaza, Hotel of the Fiery Dragon ... you're right, Bellagio. But wouldn't they do this without taking our statue?"

" They could," Bellagio replies, "but it just provides a larger advantage. Think of it: When someone chooses to go on a holiday, will they come here or will they go to the city where we live?"

" That depends," Casper says.

" On what?"

" On whether they want a beach, a historic town, or a shopping center."

" Right, but now, this place has it all. What do you think the main sight will be on all the postcards, in everyone's picture album, and in all the magazines? This enormous monument, naturally!"

Casper and Bellagio talk about the matter for another hour, searching for anything on the map and reasoning together while attempting to come to a conclusion as of who has the biggest motive and who would make the most money by having a monopoly with the big dragon statue.

They find nothing.

" It's getting late," Casper finally says. "We'll discuss it in the early morning. Let's go to sleep."

" I want to head out actually," Bellagio says.

" To do what?"

" You know, hit the night clubs, hang out in the city ... that type of stuff."

" Be my guest, man," Casper says. "I am not into those things."

Bellagio leaves the hotel and goes to one of the little restaurants. The restaurant has lots of men and women who are talking away and having a good time. One of the men approaches him and asks, "And who might you be, Mr. stranger? I've never seen you here before. Are you a tourist?"

" Uhm ... yes, a tourist. That's what I am. My name is Bellagio."

" Well, Bellagio, it's great to have you here, particularly after our little upgrade with the statue."

They start talking and become best pals. Bellagio is doing his best to get as much information out of this guy as possible. He figures that doing research requires a lot more than just searching the actual crime scene or becoming obsessed with documents and maps. The reality, the people ... they know what's going on; that's what Bellagio thinks. Then, after some social or small talk and some twenty minutes of talking, the guy across from him says something fascinating.

" You know, this monument is only helpful for the exceptionally wealthy. We do not all gain from it."

" Why not?" Bellagio asks.

" Have you heard of that guy Ragnar? He owns about 90% of the hotels here. That's right; he's the fortunate winner in this game."

" Really?" Bellagio says. "How interesting."

" Yeah, have you heard of that rumor from recently?" another guy says.

" What rumor are you talking about?"

" They say he made the 'Shining Star' monument vanish completely in one night. Scary stuff, man. It's crazy."

" Even more interesting," Bellagio says softly. He figures he knows enough and says goodbye to these men, after which he goes back to the hotel.

When he gets to the hotel, something is wrong. His intuition, as you will, informs him that he needs to rush it. He reaches his room and learns that the door is open. The window is open as well, but there is no one there.

" Casper!" he shouts.

" Bellagio, is that you?"

" Casper, what are you doing on the balcony?"

" I was attacked. Some people with weapons came in here, but before they were here, I heard them in the corridor and I hid on the terrace, hoping that they would just leave without looking there."

" Do you know where they went?"

" They must still be in the hallway. I am surprised you didn't see them when you were there."

" Okay," Bellagio says. "Let's see if we can find them."

" Are you insane? Didn't you hear me? They have weapons."

" I have one too, but we do not want to get in a fight with them. We just want to follow them."

" Ah, now that's more like it."

No sooner said than done, Bellagio gets the weapon out of his suitcase, and the duo runs to the hallway, where they see some men with sunglasses and weapons walking there. Bellagio and Casper hide behind a corner and sometimes look around it.

" I think they're leaving," Bellagio says. "Let's see where they are going."

They follow the men at a distance, out the hotel doors, through the narrow city streets, and into a big barn. They hide behind some dog crates and watch as the men report what happened to their employer.

" Sorry, Sir," one of the men says. "We couldn't find them."

" Where did they go? Unbelievable. I feel in my bones that those two men are here to determine who took the statue. I think I recognized them."

" Did you see them when you took it, boss?"

" No, but I know they work there as detectives. Oh well ... you morons couldn't even find them? Then ignore it. Leave me alone."

" But, sir ..."

" Now!"

The men leave the barn and the big boss is left to himself. Bellagio winks at Casper and signals to follow him. Gradually, they walk around crates and get closer. Unexpectedly, Bellagio gets out of his hiding place.

" Hold it right there," he says while pointing the gun at the one in charge.

" Ah, the great detective Bellagio has come to get his monument back," he says. "Do you have any idea who I am?"

" I was about to ask you," Bellagio says.

" I am Ragnar. I own nearly every hotel in this city. I could easily snap my fingers and have a hundred men show up here and detain you."

" I would shoot you before you would blink," Bellagio says.

" What do you want?" Ragnar asks.

" I want to know where the monument is, and I want the pearl."
Ragnar takes a blue-green thing out of his pocket and asks, "Oh, you mean this item? Here, catch!"
Ragnar tosses the pearl at Bellagio.
" No! Don't catch it!" Casper yells, who leaps in front of him and gets the pearl instead. Poooof!
Casper is gone, and the pearl falls on the ground.
" You evil snake! Where did you teleport him to, huh?"
" Oh, let's just say that he is being transported to a good swim in the bay area."
" Why would you send him there?"
" It's one of the first places I thought of, it has sharks, and it's close to the monument you're searching for. I do not mind telling you that, because you'll never find it in this huge city! Ha-ha-ha-ha!"
" I should kill you right here," Bellagio says.
" Go ahead. Let's see where it gets you. A court case? Prison? Do it, Bellagio. Shoot me."
Bellagio really wishes to kill this jerk, but he understands he can't just get away with it. So instead, he picks up the pearl and runs off. He does not care if any of Casper's men follow him; all he wants, is to save his pal. Bellagio runs as quick as he can to the docks in the bay area. He shows up after about 20 minutes.
" Casper!" he yells. "Casper!"
" Bellagio!"
After a few minutes, Bellagio sees Casper swimming back to the coast. He is having a hard time to get breath, but he swims as quick as he can.
" Get out of there, Casper!" Bellagio shouts. "There are sharks!"
" I know. I know. I haven't seen any of them yet," Casper says. "I think I am lucky."
Bellagio looks at Casper, who is soaking wet.
" Ha-ha! I almost thought you would become shark supper, Casper."
" I need to tell you, that this was among the creepiest experiences ever. I caught that pearl, and all of a sudden, I landed in the sea. Did you happen to get it?"
" I did, and thanks to you, I was able to."
" Well, I guess I would have had it if it would have hit you, but then I needed to come get you out of the water."
" True."
" Any idea what we should do now?" Casper asks.
" The monument should be near hear. We should search for it."
" How do you know?"
" Ragnar told me," Bellagio says.
" Wait. He just told you? Don't you think that's a way to distract you?"
" I do not think he understands who he's dealing with," Bellagio says. "Come on. Let's walk around a bit."
The two of them start inspecting the structures near the docks. For an hour or 2, they wander around, not exactly sure where to find what they're searching for. It's the middle of the night, and both of them are getting tired, but Bellagio encourages Casper not to give up, secretly encouraging himself to hang in there himself.
" How about that one?" Casper asks after a while.

" That could be something," Bellagio replies. "Let's go check it out."
In front of them is a substantial warehouse, numerous feet high, suspicious, to say the least, of hiding a tall statue like the one from their hometown. The warehouse is dark; it looks deserted. They slip into the back entrance, breaking it open after kicking at it. Bellagio understands it's prohibited to do so, but he validates it by saying that the monument is probably worth millions and the door lock just a few dollars.
When they get in, they can barely believe it.
" It's 'The Shining Star,'" Bellagio says. "Look, I bet you he had his staff members build this warehouse and after that, he teleported it over here."
" Wow. I know how it happened," Casper says, "but it's still hard to imagine how it is even possible to move an item this big into a closed area."
" But now it's going back," Bellagio says. Without being reluctant, he grabs the pearl out of his pocket and tosses it at the enormous statue.
Poooooooof!!!!
The statue vanishes and the pearl falls on the ground. Bellagio and Casper walk towards the pearl and pick it up. Bellagio puts it back into his pocket.
" Okay, can we get out of this town now?" Casper asks. "It's dark outside, it's early in the morning of the next day, and the owner of the biggest hotel chains has already sent his punks after us to kill us."
" Ha-ha! Are you scared?" Bellagio asks.
" Not really, no. Just trying to be safe."
" You're right though. We have nothing else to do here. We already teleported the monument back to its place, so we can leave."
" Good."
" Wait. Now that I think about it, there may be one more thing I want to do ..."

The morning that day, Bellagio and Casper are back at the workplace. They are both 4 hours late, since they haven't slept much. Bellagio is still rubbing his eyes.

" What's up, men?" he asks.

" Well, look who finally decided to show up. Did you know the monument is back?" one of the colleagues asks.

Bellagio understands that no one is aware of his departure with Casper, and that they are still surprised by the abrupt reappearance of the big statue. And for some reason, he does not feel like revealing all the secrets they have discovered, so he just plays along. He figures he ought to tell his manager but let the rest of them stay oblivious.

" You don't say?" Bellagio says with a smirk on his face.

" No, seriously. It just came back last night. Where were you?"

" Sleeping, duh!" Bellagio lies.

" Anyway, you missed a huge news flash. Darcy County has lost 50% of their hotels. That rich guy, named Ragnar, has suffered major losses. His hotels unexpectedly vanished and he will not tell the media what he thinks has happened."

" Interesting," Bellagio says. "Sounds like a weird story if you ask me. I mean, seriously, how can hotels disappear, just like that?"

Casper laughs. He knows that Bellagio is just pretending that he doesn't know anything, but they both know very well what happened. Bellagio looks at Casper, who shakes his head and smiles before he walks to his coworker, puts his hand on his shoulder and says, "Listen, Bobby. There are some things that will always stay a secret, no matter how much you search for the truth. It's just one of those magic things in life, don't you think, Bellagio?"

" Absolutely," Bellagio concurs. "I do not think we'll ever find out where those hotels got teleport ... I mean what happened to those hotels."

THE END

Secrets from the Underworld

Entry 1: The Tricks

I looked at the clock and saw the time. I was already getting late. I had to rush. I instantly took my jacket, my wallet, my key, and my sunglasses; I never forgot my sunglasses.

I ran outside and hopped into my car. I started the engine, looked into my mirror, turned on my blinker, and got out of the car park. I checked the speed limit of the road again. Oh yes, it was only 25 miles per hour in this zone. Aaaargh! That wasn't going to help me arrive fast. I was hoping the commissioner would not be too hard on me.

Late. I was late, but it didn't seem to matter, because the commissioner, the big chief of the police station, came to me and gave me a warm welcome.

" Agent Oliver," he said, "good to see you."

He shook my hand and put his left hand on my shoulder. I looked him into the eyes and showed him a smile, rather sheepish, and after that I followed him to his office. Obviously, he had something crucial for me to do.

" Oliver, we have a serious issue," he said when he sat me down in front of his desk.

" I'm listening," I said.

He sat down himself and leaned forward. "There are corrupt cops among us."

I raised my eyebrows. "That's a serious accusation, Commissioner. Do you have any evidence to back that statement up?"

" I don't," he said. "That's where you come in. We've seen some things that look suspicious, but we can't put our finger on it. We need you to go sort it out. Learn who it is and what they want."

" But, Sir, corruption comes in a lot of forms if you think about it. What do you suspect they are doing?"

" We don't know precisely, like I said, but we found evidence that someone has been tampering with the lock in the storage room."

" Okay, I will look into it," I said.

When I left his office, I instantly went to the designated place. The storage room had lots of stuff. It had not been cleaned up in a while, but the door was always locked, except... for this time ...

The first thing I discovered, was that somebody had forced him- or herself in here. They kind of broke the lock but that person tried to made it appear like absolutely nothing had happened by connecting it sloppily. The most important question was: What did they take?

I turned on the light, and I looked at the mess. It was like the cops would just seize products and then discard them here without looking back or researching them. It came to me that we needed a system, something we could depend on. But right now, it was more crucial to find out what was missing.

I was amazed at the things I saw there, like a damaged shotgun, a spear, a shovel, a sword, a pack of balloons, a container, 2 bottles of pop, and a copier. But something stuck out.

" What the ...?" I said. "What is that?"

It was a violin. It had a reddish-brown color, and some sort of decor on it. I wondered who would have taken a violin. It didn't seem like a dangerous or suspicious object to me. What was so sketchy about a violin that they had to bring it in? Unusual.

I kept looking thoroughly, skimming the surface of the shelves, trying to find any sign of something that had been moved, taken, or touched.

" Aha!" I said after a while. "Something was here, and now it's gone. I will alert the commissioner."

But when I went to his workplace, he was reluctant.

" It's better if people do not know that I am associated with this case," he said. You need to be really sly about it."

" But I don't know what used to be there. I can see the difference. The dust is blown away. Someone took something from that spot. Could you please come take a look?"

" Well, all right," the commissioner said.

He followed me to the storage room and asked me where there was something missing.

" Over there," I said.

" Oh," he said. "I think there was some sort of device there. I never knew what it was. They brought it in because somebody was bothering the neighbors with the sounds that originated from it. But they never finished the research. The guy who had it, moved away, and the officers at the workplace forgot it."

" If someone took it, then it must be necessary," I said.

" You're right. I suggest you check out the computer and see if you can find any records of it being taken."

That's what I was going to do.

I turned the computer system on. It took forever!

" Huh!" I sighed. "Come on, silly piece of scrap. Hurry up. I don't have all the time."

A coworker stood behind me. "Impatient with the computer system, huh? What are you looking up?" he asked.

" Uhm ... actually nothing specifically," I said. "I just needed to find an address."

I didn't want to tell him what I was looking into, because every policeman or -woman in the bureau was a suspect. When you know that it's one of the officers at the police headquarters, it's better not to trust your coworkers and let them in on the little tricks you're discovering.

Ultimately, I began the right program and looked at what had disappeared. There was an unclear picture of a little machine with several buttons, but it was too blurry to tell what it actually was. The description just had a question mark; nothing more. I figured I wouldn't learn anything from the recorded file somebody had put into the computer. If only they were a bit more precise here at the bureau.

I looked around me with suspicious eyes. Which of these policemen stole the device my commissioner was talking about? And what was the device for anyway? At first, I considered questioning some people at the police headquarters, but I didn't know whom to trust and I didn't want to let anyone know I was on this case.

I closed my eyes and leaned back in my chair. Since we operated in cubicles, the others didn't see me doing that, or they probably would have discussed my laziness.

But I wasn't being lazy.

I was listening. My senses sharpened. I was observing everything that was happening around me. There were ticking noises by people who were typing on their keyboards, clicking sounds by others who were using their computer mouse, people talking, noises from automobiles that were barely audible through the thick double pane windows, and a lot more.

I overheard their discussions. Some men were discussing their weekends, while others were submitting reports or going over parking and speeding tickets, or going over the police policies.

I let my thoughts circulate. I wanted my body to unwind but focus intensely at the same time. I knew that whenever I did this, I would get some type of inspiration from beyond. It was strange how it worked. Ideas flashed through my mind, a partnership of the countless impulses that had entered my brain without being processed.

Something stood apart.

What was that?

I heard a noise of ... of ...

I couldn't put my finger on it, but it was right beside me. I opened my eyes and stood up. I looked around me and saw it. One of my coworkers was shaking something.

" What's that?" I asked.

" What's what?" he asked me.

" That noise. What are you doing?"

" Oh. This? That's just me shaking the whiteout. I made a mistake on a paper and I can't remove it, because I wrote it with a pen. So I'm just fixing it."

" Genius," I said.

" Huh?"

" Never mind. Thanks," I said, and I ran away from the desk.

For some reason, the shaking of the whiteout bottle told me something. It connected dots in my mind to white fluids and white powder, and after that, I knew that I hadn't tried to use powder yet. I had not tried to search for fingerprints yet ...

Entry 3: Chasing

There I was, at the forensics office. I knew I could find the equipment I needed to look for fingerprints. I snuck therein, chuckling inside about the absence of security they had. The people who worked at forensics weren't into all the action. All they did, was research study products and profiles and such. I considered them to be somewhat geeky, but hey, it was me who was going to share that same nerdiness by getting the right tools to do the job.

I looked around and found what I needed. Then I went back into the storage room. I applied the white dust for the suspicious spots where the machine should have been.

" Aha!" I thought. "That must be a finger print."

I used my brush to get the needed results and took some pictures of what I found. I was so curious that I practically forgot to close the door and take my stuff with me. I took the electronic camera and placed the chip into the computer at my desk. I inspected it. The other police officers were all too busy. I typed in a few things and did a search. After a long time of loading, the computer system revealed a match.

" Bingo," I quietly said to myself. "I got him."

In front of me, on the computer system screen, I saw a familiar face. It was a coworker called Dolleph Candice. I never spoke to him much. I mean, there were numerous officers at this police headquarters, so I didn't get to know everybody. But I had seen him around. He probably worked at another department or something. But where was he now?

I thought I could ask some colleagues without raising suspicions that I was working on a specific case, so I did.

" Hey Charlie, do you know where Dolleph Candice went?"

" Dolleph? No, haven't seen him."

" Lewis, have you seen him?" I asked another coworker.

" Dolleph Candice? What do you need him for? I thought he worked upstairs."

" Okay, thanks."

I went upstairs and asked around some more. One of the officers at that department said he had seen him run out the door with a maker, but he didn't know where he went. It was pointless to look for him in the huge city, so instead, I went to the commissioner's workplace. He welcomed me, but he wasn't extremely pleased to see me.

" Didn't I tell you to be discrete? Others should not know you are working with me on a case."

" Oh, it does not matter anymore," I said. "I already know who stole the device from the storage."

" Really? How?"

" I dusted the place for finger prints and there was only one match: Dolleph Candice."

" Weiss ..." the commissioner said. "What happened to him?"

" I do not know, but I want to find out. I need access to his computer system files."

" You got it," the commissioner said.

He searched for the password for Dolleph's computer. We both went to his cubicle and turned it on. Others were just doing their own thing. We didn't stick out. The two of us waited until the computer started running its primary programs.

" Stupid piece of scrap," the commissioner grumbled. "Does it always take this long?"

" Yes, it does, Sir. My computer system is just as slow."

" I'm sorry, Oliver. I will see if we can get faster ones sometime. Today, our budget is pretty limited. Man, exactly how long is this going to take? This is so absurd!"

I chuckled a little inside when I saw that I wasn't the only one losing my temper when working on these slow computers. When we were finally done waiting, we looked into Dolleph's files. We browsed and searched, and eventually, we found something intriguing.

" These are some data from the old factory outside of town," I said. "Look. It has an address, pictures, and e-mails to the power plant to get electrical power going there. I wonder what he is doing there."

" Hooking up that device, certainly," the commissioner said.

" What shall we do?" I asked. "Send a system there?"

" No. There are numerous things that need our attention. We cannot afford to just send out a bunch of people over there without even knowing if he is at that structure."

" Do you want me to go on my own? I can do that."

" No, not on your own," the commissioner said. "I will go with you."

" Sir?"

" I haven't been out in the field for a long period of time. It's time for me to get back into action. Don't stress over all my other tasks. They will wait on me till I return."

I chuckled. "Sounds great, Sir. It's all up to you."

The commissioner and I hopped into a patrol car and headed towards the borders of the city. When we came there, we inspected the address again. It was clear which building was being used, because the old enterprise zone outside the city center was deserted; yet there was only one structure in which the lights were on.

" See that?" the commissioner asked. "There is our rat. Let's get him."

We jumped out of the car and got in the garage. It was totally empty. It was like going into some ruins from a few a century ago. Bricks were broken, plants were growing on several parts of the structure, and the mold smell penetrated our senses as quickly as we stepped foot into the edifice. We looked around and found the stairs to the top of the factory. Without being reluctant, we ran up the stairs. The commissioner told me to pull my weapon and did the same. As we approached the upper floor, we slowed down and ended up being more alert. We had no idea what we would find there.

Suddenly, we heard a voice. "You can come in! I already saw you when you pulled your car up!"

We went into a huge room, practically as huge as the parking lot on the base floor. It had windows on all sides, and it hadn't been demolished yet. There were some chairs and tables in the corners, but what caught our eye was the person on the far end of the room, who was holding a device that looked like a remote control. He was in a police uniform and had a big grin on his face. He was holding a revolver in his other hand, pointing it at us. We closed in and listened to what he had to say.

" You will witness the best moment in history," he said.

" Dolleph?" the commissioner asked. "What are you doing?"

" I am glad you ask," he said, "but before I continue, I need to ask you to drop your weapons."

" And why would we do that?" I asked. "You took something from the bureau. Why would we trust you?"

" Because I am willing to share the profits with you," Dolleph said.

" Of what?" I asked.

" Of everything. Everything! You see, this gadget here ... it's a trigger. That machine over there is a real sonar system. It sends audible waves through the air and alerts the creatures who will help me eliminate the whole city."

" Hold on, hold on," I said. "What creatures? And why would you erase the entire city?"

" Oh, come on," Dolleph said. "What do you think? Money, duh. If I kill everyone in this town, all that there is left, is for me to take all the cash from the corpses, from the bank, and from every home."

" You evil, mean, self-centered ..." the commissioner said.

" Whoa, let's not start calling names," Dolleph said. "I am being extremely generous here. I am willing to split with you. You can each have 33%. Fair is fair. What do you say, men?"

" Never," the commissioner said.

" Just out of interest," I started, "how are you going to eliminate the city? What creatures are you speaking about?"

" Ghosts, my friends ... ghosts. Let me clarify. This device reaches all the way to the depths of the Underworld. When I press this button here, they will come and damage everything within a 100-mile radius. All I have to do, is hide myself in that vault over there, and then I will be safe. Within 24 hours, they'll be done and I can come out to get what I deserve."

" You will do no such thing," the commissioner said, as he came closer with his gun.

" Lower your weapons, or I will make it go off," Dolleph said.

" You're going to do that anyway!" I shouted. "What's the point?! Now, put the remote down or we WILL shoot you!"

" I am giving you one last chance here," Dolleph said. "If you shoot me, I will still press the button on the remote and the ghosts will come get you. Put the GUNS DOWN!!!"

I was tired of all this threatening. I glanced at the commissioner. He didn't trust it for one bit. I stopped thinking and pulled the trigger.

BAM!

I hit the hand in which Dolleph held the push-button control.

" Aaaargh!"

Screaming in pain, he dropped the remote and fell on his knees. But before we could do anything, he reached for the remote with his other hand and pushed the button.

" Noooooo!" I shouted.

Entry 5: Don't Be So Careless

The next thing we realized, we felt a little vibration and it was practically like there was some sort of high-pitched noise that was tough to hear for us as humans.
" You cannot stop it. Ha-ha-ha-ha-ha!" Dolleph yelled. He tried to run away with the remote in his hand, and he almost reached one of the doors. But then the commissioner did his share.
BAM! BAM! BAM! BAM!
Dolleph got hit. The commissioner had shot him and Dolleph was dead. We looked at him for a few seconds, feeling a little uncomfortable. We had wanted to solve this in a non-violent way, but he had left us no choice. Besides, the problem wasn't resolved yet. The vibrating machine was still sending out waves through the air, notifying all the ghosts in the Underworld, or so we were told.
" Turn it off," the commissioner said.
I walked towards the device and shot it.
BAM! BAM!
2 bullets sufficed to make it stop. Smoke originated from the device. It was broken. That resolved that. Dolleph was definitely taken out of the equation. But were the ghosts still coming?
We kept an eye out the window. In the beginning, we didn't see anything. The horizon was empty and everything appeared to be safe. But after a few minutes, we saw little swarms in the distance; swarms of flying creatures that moved differently than any birds we had ever seen.
" That must be them," the commissioner said. "What are we going to do?"
" Kill as many of them as we can," I said, but I knew that would not suffice to stop them. It looked like there were thousands of them.
" Any ideas of how to destroy countless ghosts simultaneously?" I asked.
" With an army maybe," the commissioner said. "This is awful. People will die. We have to do something."
" Let's go to the police headquarters," I suggested.
" Good idea."
We ran down and entered into our car. As we drove to the police station, we found, to our horror, that we were too late. Ghosts were already flying in between the skyscrapers, shooting citizens with their fireballs and flying around to blow things up. People were shouting. There was chaos everywhere. Some of the city's residents were combating ghosts, others were hiding, and the majority of them were just aimlessly running for their lives. The explosive sounds were heard all over; it was a complete disaster.
" We're almost there," the commissioner said. "We need to get all officers to collaborate and stay together. Only then do we stand a chance."
We steered through the mayhem and evaded some big explosions and fireballs the beasts were gushing at us. I shot a few of them with my gun, and the commissioner used his best driving abilities to get us to our destination. When we got here, we saw the panic in the police headquarters too. Cops were running around, unintentionally knocking over papers, and many of them were on the phone with scared citizens.

I stood there, surprised by the situation. Ghosts were all across the city and there were only a handful of police officers. I just hoped that those flying spooks wouldn't do too much damage with their attacks before we could head out there and start resisting them. The commissioner was doing everything in his power to organize the police. But then I walked by the storage room.

" Hey," I said. "Perhaps the ... nah, that would not do anything."

Entry 6: The Violin

I opened the door and had a vision.

It was almost like an epiphany, a musing from on high. It hit me like lightning. I can't truly explain what it felt like, but I will do my best to put it into words. I felt calm and serene, as if nothing wrong was going to take place.

I closed my eyes and felt myself floating away towards the sky. I watched the city and observed the panic everywhere. The ghosts were flying around, causing traffic accidents and damage in all the corners of our giant metropolis. But then they disappeared. I heard a sweet sound, lower than some type of squeaking but high enough to pierce through the very fibers of my soul. A thousand thoughts and memories flashed before my eyes, until I opened them and woke up with a shock.

In front of me was the violin, the unusual item somebody had taken and probably never reported.

" There must be more to this thing. Maybe this is not just some regular musical instrument," I said as I walked closer.

I picked up the bow and started playing. It was insane! It was as if my arms and hands were managed by one of the most brilliant brains in deep space, although I knew that wasn't me. But it was me! How did I do that?

I watched my limbs play a beautiful work of art I had never even heard before. It went quicker, and before I knew it, the noise was as if an entire orchestra was backing me up. I kept playing and going on for 10 minutes that time.

Then I bowed, for some reason, feeling that others were watching me. It was the strangest thing ever, like being hypnotized but still being able to manage myself in some way.

When I was done playing, I put the violin down and looked at it.

" Wow," I said. "What is with that thing? Is this some sort of magical thing or something?"

As I gazed at it, it dawned on me how stupid this question was. Obviously, it was magic! I just played a masterpiece I didn't even know.

" Wake up, stupid," I said to myself.

Then I snapped out of it and realized we were still in a dire situation. I needed to go join the ranks and start eliminating some ghosts with the other policemen. What was I doing here playing a violin?

I ran towards the hallway of the police headquarters and was stunned when I came there.

Entry 7: Ending Everything

The police officers were standing there with their mouths open; some inside the hallway, others in front of the building. When it began to sink in what they were so astonished about, I, too, opened my mouth and looked at the city with big eyes.
All the ghosts were gone.
People were still in shock, and there was still some mayhem by running individuals, little accidents, and some who were still in survival mode; but the ghosts were gone. The ghosts were gone!!!
" What happened?" I asked the commissioner.
" I don't know," he said as he kept staring.
Then he shook his head to snap out of it and return to reality. "Okay, everyone. We still have work to do. The ghosts may be gone, but the city is still in turmoil. Let's get to it. You, you, and you! Go to the downtown location. You go to the West Neighborhood, and you three come with me. Let's go! Let's go! Let's go!"
We all separated and tried to calm the metaphorical storm by assuring people that the risk was gone, resolve arguments and do the needed work for collisions and lost or harmed goods. It was a lot of work and it took us four days to get everything completed. Practically every policeman and -woman was out in the field or on the phone all the time. Luckily, we got paid and were thanked for our overtime.
Ultimately, when the peace in the city had been restored, I went into the commissioner's workplace. He welcomed me with a smile, shook my hand, and took a seat. "Everything is back to the way it used to be," he said.
" I am glad that it is, Sir."
" It's odd," he said. "The ghosts were assaulting everyone, but somehow, they got frightened, disgusted, or shut off by something. They all stiffened a little, even when flying, and then left in a hurry. What do you think that is, Officer?"
" I have no idea, Sir."
" Really? Because someone told me you were playing the violin in the storeroom at the exact moment they began flying away. Let me ask you this, Officer, why did you start playing that instrument when there were a lot of people to be helped and ghosts to be killed?"
" Honestly, Sir, I don't know. It was as if something triggered me to do so."
" Well, I do not know how you did it, and I don't know whatever powers that odd violin possesses, but I am convinced that you playing it relates to their flight. By the way, the reports state that there were zero fatalities amongst the citizens."
" Wow. That's wonderful news, and yes it could be associated with it," I admitted.
" And that's why I have determined to give you a promotion at the job," the commissioner said.
" Oh, thank you, Sir. But what if the events weren't related?"
" Then I guess you were just lucky and it was just a coincidence, but I'll give you the promotion in that case anyway."
He winked at me and told me to leave.
I wondered later on if he secretly knew about the magic powers of the violin, but I never asked him if he did.

THE END

Mobsters and Moping

Entry 1: Staying Calm

I do not want to sound too dramatic here, but I quit.
I just recently quit the business.
I was never sure about it in the first place, but now I know I made the right decision.
When it was time, it just struck me: I had to stop doing this. I can't make up for everything I did wrong and I am not happy with my past transgressions, but now I feel better. I have released myself from the bonds that were dragging me down the drain.
What am I referring to here, right?
Well, let me clarify it a little. I actually worked at a crime organization. There were weapons and drugs and smugglers and killers. It was a dark underground movement: The mob.
It all started with my family. My dad was in the business, so I was simply being prepared to take control of it after his death ... which could be anytime, because people were murdering each other constantly. You never knew when your life was going to be over.
Initially, I had no idea what was going on. You know, like a kid, just hopping along with his father, relying on the fact that his deeds were proper and justified. But as I matured, I discovered increasingly more it that turned me away from it. I began hating it, but I actually stayed it, partly because I was afraid they would kill me if I would leave.
On the other hand, I took some notes about things I learned when you're in an unlawful business, but then again, I think they would actually apply to anybody's life.
Let me explain what happened on that rainy day when everything failed when my Italian family was stressing over absolutely nothing.
" Antoni!" my father shouted.
" What's wrong, dad?" I asked.
" Did you do what I asked? You were supposed to have the stuff ready to go an hour ago."
" I'm sorry, dad. It won't happen again."
" Yeah, yeah. Just get it prepared now and you're good."
" Sure, dad."
I got the machine in the car that my dad had mentioned; it was a machine that can block any lasers and alarm, and therefore providing us a safe way through any building we wanted to get into. The only thing we had to look out for, was that we wouldn't be seen and/or recognized.
We always wore hats. And although I still do not know why exactly, I just copied everybody else's habits. I loved my hat and I loved the suit I would usually wear.
Perhaps they did it to look fancy or wealthy, and perhaps they did it to somewhat cover their faces when they needed to in order to avoid being seen. I don't know, but they all did it. The whole mob did it.
I got the car all set, meaning that I put the device in it and drove it in front of the big home all of us resided in.
" What are we going to steal this time, dad?" I asked in innocence.
" Not steal, child ... seize. We are going to confiscate a golden apple."
" Why would we take a golden apple? You can't even eat those."
" True, but you can get a truckload of money for one. Right guys? Heh heh ..."

My dad chuckled first, but I saw soon that the 4 other people with hats and suits made sure to laugh about his silly jokes. They would not dare stand up to him. It was always like that. You do not talk back to your boss; but my dad was not the big boss. There was another one above him. It was an easy matter of hierarchy. He would need to report to another guy above him.

And where was I?

Way at the bottom.

That's why I was preparing the car for our "little trip."

" Move in, boys," my dad said. "We are about to peel a heavy apple, if you know what I mean."

The others chuckled. Another dumb joke. Oh well, I didn't mind it. It wasn't my dad I grew tired of. It was the entire organization, the corruption, and the moral predicaments I had to deal with after a while.

We got in the car and drove towards a museum with high security innovation. I was curious to find out if our device would work here too, since it probably had its defects. We drove to the other side of the street. It was late at night, so that the hats definitely covered half of our faces with their shadows, something that would be convenient if anybody tried to find us and arrest us later on.

The heavy rain was covering our identity much more and discouraging people from hanging out in this public spot.

" We go to the side. There is a fire escape there that I know how to open without making a sound," my dad said.

We snuck around the side, jumping over a few hedges, and walking past a fountain. We looked for guards but found none. Obviously, no one felt like being outside in this dreadful weather. Or perhaps they thought the alarm system was good enough to keep them informed of any burglars. Fascinating ... was that going to stop our machine from working? I hoped not. I didn't want to be getting caught.

" Let's go over here," my dad whispered to the others. He jumped over another bush, but because it was slippery, he felt flat on his face.

" Ouch!"

I saw a small propensity in the others to be laughing, but they controlled themselves and held it in. One of the men looked the other way, probably to avoid being caught with a smile. It was funny ... crazy actually, but they weren't supposed to make fun of their boss, so they refrained from doing so.

" Will one of you idiots help me up?" my dad asked.

" Sorry, boss."

" No problem, boss."

In the meantime, I was dragging the notorious device to the side door and awaiting further instructions. My dad limped over to me and took a crowbar out of this coat. The others looked at him and were waiting on his next move.

" Wait," I said. "That's your genius strategy? A basic crowbar? Won't that sound the alarm?"

" Of course not. You see this? This will work more wonders than that expensive innovation of yours. Turn on the device and we'll be even safer. It will work; trust me."

I put the machine down and turned it on. Vibrating waves originated from the technological wonder, blocking the electrical pulses the opening door would send to the alarm. My dad opened the door as I watched the device shock everything and shake up and down.

CLING!

The door opened.

All of us waited.

We stood there with our mouths open, looking at the door that was so easily opened by this break-in professional.

" Wow, dad. That was quick," I said.

" Thanks, child. One day, you'll be a pro like me. Now let's go inside."

The alarm didn't go off. I was relieved. We went through the corridor and snuck into the main hall.

" What are you being so silent for?" my dad said after a while. "There's no one here. See? Helloooooo!"

I wasn't too comfortable with my dad being like that. Was he challenging fate? Why couldn't he just be a little more cautious about this? I mean, wouldn't it be better to take a little extra care and be more mindful? What if there was a security guard?

" What are you looking at, child? There is no danger. We'll just enter and get the golden apple."

His attitude was driving me nuts, but I was stuck with him and he was still my dad. We opened another door, a bigger one this time. There it was!

It was the golden apple! But what was that glow around it? What was going on with the purple radiance around it? It didn't appear regular.

" Uhm ... dad," I stuttered. "Do you really think it's a great idea to steal that apple? There's something strange about it."

" So?" he asked. "A little radiance never hurt anybody. Let's go get it. Go, men. Now!"

Everyone went to the apple to check it out. It was lovely and glossy. There was a glass bowl around it. Without thinking twice, my dad pushed the others aside and raised the bowl.

THAT was a big mistake.

It triggered the alarm.

Weeeeooooweeeoooh!

The alarm was louder than the highest volume of my portable music playing device, and although my young ears had been damaged by limitless rock and opera music, I still put my fingers in my ears to silence the loud noises.

Weeeeooooweeeooh!

Everybody stressed out. They ran in all different directions but could not go anywhere. Two of the men ran into each other and fell on the floor. My dad grabbed the apple and put it in his pocket, after which his pocket started to glow.

" Weird," he said.

I looked around us. There were four doors that had led us to this room, but now they were all shut by thick metal doors, which fell down instantly when the alarm began, stopping us from leaving the room.

" What are we going to do?" I exclaimed. "We are trapped! How are we gonna get out of here?"

" Stay calm," my dad said. "There is always a way."

I was amazed by his self-confidence but I doubted his reasoning. What if there was no other way out?

We looked around and thought of a plan to leave before the police would get here. Everything was completely closed.
Everything ...
Except for the air shafts.
" There!" my dad said as he pointed to one of them. "That's our way out. See? I told you it would be all right. We can just climb through those."
He ran towards the air shaft and pulled the lattice off. The others ran towards him, even the ones who had bonked heads. They followed him into the air shaft and crawled through the narrow spaces. I was last, and I regret to say that I didn't even want to go. It was scary and I didn't know where it was leading us, but I didn't appear to have any other option, so I just did as they did.
After a few turns, we got there in the corridor where we went into the structure. I was happy when I discovered that the outside door had not been rocked by a similar steel door. There was nothing holding us back from running outside.
So we did.
We ran outside and looked around us to find the fastest route to the car. In the meantime, the alarm was still making noise.
Weeoooweeooweeooo!
" Let's go!" my dad said. "We have no time to lose. Follow me."
We ran through the storm. The loud thunder was covering the loud noises of the police vehicles that had just stopped in front of the museum. Fortunately none of them were near our car, and they all ran in the wrong direction: Straight to the front entryway.
My dad, who was soaking wet by now, looked to the side and sad enthusiastically, "See boys? They went to the wrong door. Ha-ha!"
The other men weren't too certain about whether to laugh. Was it a real joke or was he just chuckling because he was glad that he didn't get caught? They showed an awkward smirk on their faces but kept running. None of those awkward weirdoes slipped this time, but I had the feeling we forgot something.
" The machine!" I unexpectedly said as I came to a halt. "We left the machine! We need to go back!"
" No way," my dad said. "If we go back, they'll find us. They are most likely near the side entrance already. There is no time!"
" But if we leave it, they'll know that it was us who took the golden apple," I argued.
" How? How will they know? It's not like it has our name on it or something."
" Uhmm ..." one of the guys said reluctantly.
" Wait a minute. Does it?" my dad asked.
" Well, technically ..." our fellow criminal started, ".. it only has your surname on it. I saw it."
" WHAT?!!!!"
My dad yelled so loud that we saw one of the police officers look our way. Despite the heavy rain, he still heard my dad's disappointed exclamation. We all ducked. My dad got up a little to see if he was still watching us.
" Okay, the coast is clear," he said. "Sorry I lost my temper, boys. But why does it have my last name on it? Which of you belugas put my name on that device?"

They all looked up for a while. Then one of them said sheepishly, "You see, boss, when we gave it to you, we thought it would be nice to have your name engraved on it ... you know ... like a present."

My dad came closer and got him by the collar.

" You mean to say that you actually went to the store and had my name engraved on it?" he said between his teeth, holding back his rage.

" Well, yeah ... a tattoo guy. He said he would repair it for 20 bucks. You know ..."

" IDIOTS!"

Again, the police officer looked our way, but we figured his vision was fuzzy because of the evaporating rain that was falling on the ground. We ducked again. My dad was furious.

" Fine," he said after a minute. "You go get the device, son. I am sure you will have a better chance of bringing it back than these 4 imbeciles. Let's go. I will see you at home. Do not mess this up, please."

" I won't let you down, dad," I said, pretending to fully believe in myself.

I was actually edgy; I was nervous. The police officers were all over the place and I was about to go back. Sure, they all went through the front door, but one of them might have wound up outside the side door, where the machine was.

I looked around and leapt over a hedge. I looked again and jumped over another one, and another one ... every time ducking after I jumped.

Wow!

A cop just came outside and looked my way. Did he see me?

" Hey, what was that?" I heard him say.

O-oh. Not good. Not good!!!

The guard came closer and closer. I heard his footsteps and his cough as he approached me. He was only a few feet away.

" I think it came from over here!" he says to three other law enforcement officers who came out of the building.

He was standing in front of me, towering over me when I was hiding beneath the bushes, when all of a sudden ...

" Meeououw!"

A cat came out of the bush; it had clearly been hiding because of the rain, and had found a comfortable area near the hedge I was sitting. It quickly jumped up and attacked the police officer's face.

" Aah! Get out of my face, foolish cat!" the officer yelled.

He threw the scratching cat on the ground and looked around him.

" I guess it was just a cat!" he shouted to the other men.

That was close. The cat had saved my life. I should go to it and shake its paw.

However, there were more vital matters: The machine was still there. I couldn't let them find it. So I waited till the officer was gone and snuck towards the area where we had left it. It was still there. Great. I lifted the device up and transported it out of there. Within minutes, I had the ability to get the device far from the building without getting spotted. It was pretty heavy, so I needed to take a break.

I was panting heavily when I saw my dad drive by in his car, along with the men he had been so mad at.

" Glad you made it out alive, kid. Now, let's go before the police sees us."

I do not think I had ever been happier to see my dad than at that time. I lifted the device and put it in the car, after which I took a seat and my dad hit the gas pedal.

Vroooom!

Again, that was close ... we almost got caught. I looked at the others. They had ruined it and my dad knew it. They didn't dare looking me in the eyes. One of them didn't have to anyway, since he was wearing sunglasses.

" So where did you get the name printed?" I asked.

No response.

" Oh, come on," I said. "I returned and laid my life down the line to get this device. Now I wish to know why."

They looked at each other and probably thought they ought to respond, because a few seconds after that, one of them said, "It's on the other side. See?"

I turned the device around. He was right. It was on the other side. But then I discovered something terrible.

" Hold on," I said. "This is the bottom."

" Yeah, so?" one of them asked.

" So?!!! Well, let me tell you why that is an issue, guys. The bottom was on the floor. See this engraving with our last name? Now there is a print in the sand with our surname. The police will look around and find our name printed in the sand."

" But it will be backwards," the guy with the sunglasses said. "So they won't be able to read it."

He smiled when he said it, as if he had just said something smart. I rolled my eyes and started seeing why my dad called them names all the time. They truly were idiots.

" Stop the car," I told my dad as I sighed.

" What's wrong, boy?"

I explained to my dad why I needed to go back to erase the print in the sand, and he let me out. I didn't take the machine, obviously. I didn't need that heavy weight wearing me down. My dad thought it would be best not to drive back. We were just a couple of rocks away, but we didn't want the cops to recognize our license plate. So I walked. No worries about that.

Well, I didn't walk. I ran.

I ran as quick as my legs could carry me. I looked out for cops, since they were everywhere. I hid behind trees, snuck behind bushes, and finally came to the spot where the machine had been standing, next to the side door.

There it was.

Our surname printed backwards in the sand because of the machine that had been standing there. I rapidly grabbed some mud and covered it up. No more traces, not even small ones.

At that moment, a police officer opened the side door from the inside. He didn't see me, since the door swung open against me and left me behind it.

" Let's see what's on this side," the police officer said.

He looked at the ground. I was happy that I had erased our name in the nick of time. Then he stepped outside and looked around him. There was no other way to hide now. I got there from behind the door and punched him in the face.

" Ughh!" he said as he fell to the ground.

It didn't knock him out, but I wasn't going to take him out, since I hadn't done anything like that before. So I escaped, which, when I thought about it afterwards, wasn't a clever idea at all, because as soon as the cop got up, he called his little assistants over.

" Get him!" he shouted. "He is attempting to get away!"

Within minutes, the yard was crawling with the police. I ran into all different directions, hoping they wouldn't pursue me. I hoped they would leave me alone.

They didn't.

Half a dozen polices had already seen me and were now following me, trying to run faster than I did. This was it. I was going to prison. There was no way to talk myself out of this one, and I was losing the race. I panted and ran as fast as I could, but they were literally gaining on me.

All of a sudden, a car pulled over.

It was my dad's car.

" Get in! Now!" he said. "Hurry!"

I got into the car and slammed the door, after which the tires shrieked and my dad made one of the most dangerous moves in traffic I had seen him do.

Eeeeeeeaaa!

He turned around and drove away, breaking the law in another way by surpassing the speed limit and going 30 miles over. But it got me out of there. I was safe.

" Thanks, dad," I said.

" I would never leave you behind, boy. I just realized that, which is why I came back. You owe me one."

" How about us?" the guy with the sunglasses asked.

My dad looked back. He rolled his eyes and sighed.

" We helped too, didn't we?" another guy with said from below his hat.

" You ..." he began and after that breathed in. ".. You morons are going to cook spaghetti and pizzas for the next week AND DO ALL THE DISHES !!!"

" Sorry, boss."

Entry 4: The Woman

Back at the house, my dad congratulated me for being so courageous. This was one of those moments: My dad was a good man, but he had just been drawn into all of this. I think if he would see what this organization made him do, he would understand that it would be better to step away from it.

" Son, we're going to see Antoni. He is the leader in this town. But believe me, you do not want to get in his way. If he doesn't like somebody, he will put you down."

" Oh, I can take an insult or 2," I said. "That's not an issue."

" Ha! No, you do not comprehend. When I say, 'put you down,' I mean truly put you down, like sleeping with the fishes."

" That doesn't sound great," I said.

" You're right, it does not. So you better keep your mouth shut."

" Okay, dad."

We got in the car and went to the big boss' villa on the edge of the city. It was big. The backyard had Italian statues everywhere, flower beds, and columns from the Roman age. The house itself was most likely three times as big as ours, if not more.

We walked up a few stairs and came to the front entryway. A bodyguard stood there in suit and tie, with sunglasses and a hat, just like everyone else. I do not get why the police had such a hard time finding the mobsters, because all of us looked a certain way. However, I think they shouldn't be suspicious of anybody with a hat and a suit, since lots of people walked around in those sorts of clothes back then.

" Who are you and what do you want?" the bodyguard asked.

" We are here to see Antoni. He called us here," my dad answered.

" Hold on a sec," the guard said.

We watched as he talked with someone over a little speaker gadget, with an earphone attached to his suit. He told the individual on the other side (most likely the big boss) that someone was here and requested for permission to let us in.

" The boss is fine with you coming in now," he said after a while.

He opened the door for us, and we went inside. The big hall was large and glamorous. It looked like a palace. I had no idea how this guy made so much money, but it was probably not ethical or legal. In any case, he appeared to be getting wealthy from it. That was obvious.

We walked up the red carpet on the stairs and came to the second floor, where we were let in and saw Antoni. He had a white suit and a white hat. His cigar smoke filled the room, which made me a little sick before I got used to it a bit more.

" Welcome to the palacio," he said in a thick Italian accent. "I heard you were at the museum last night. What happened there?"

" Well, we thought of taking the golden apple," my dad began.

But I didn't hear the rest, because at that moment, the door opened, and I saw the most beautiful individual I had ever seen in my life. She came in with a tray with some beverages on it and looked at me over her shoulder when she walked past me. This Italian lady had black hair, a white top and a fading green skirt. I wasn't sure if every girl in town would have said that these colors matched, but I was certain that to me, every color looked good on her.

" Oh, hi, Cynthia," the big boss said, disrupting my father. "Put the tray over there, please."
" Hi, Cynthia," I said.
Antoni didn't look happy when I said that. Cynthia looked a little worried at the big boss. Then she gave me this look as to say, "You better not speak with me in his presence." Then the managing bulldog spoke out, protecting his offspring.
" Did you just speak with my daughter?" Antoni asked. "'Cause if you are actually trying to hit on my daughter, then you can just get outta here. I don't accept that."
" Oh no, I just said 'hi.' That's all. Nothing more," I said.
" Good. Let's keep it that way," he said. "Anyway, what were you saying about the golden apple?"

The big boss listened to our adventure at the museum and demanded to see the object. My dad promised him he would bring him the radiant golden apple next time. He didn't point out that it might have secret powers, since I was the one who brought it up and it hadn't even been proven yet. After some small talk, we got out of the room. My dad went to the bathroom and I stayed in the great hall.

" Pssst ..." a voice said from around the corner.

" Cynthia?" I asked.

" What's your name?" she asked.

" I am Antoni," I said.

" Pleased to meet you. Thank you for saying 'hello,'" she said.

I felt my heart beating faster, and I am pretty sure I was blushing.

" Well, it was 'hi,'" I said, trying to correct her. By the way, later on I thought that was the stupidest thing I could have said, but it just came out.

" Hee-hee!" she giggled. "You know what? You're amusing. I like you. But I am in trouble."

" What's going on?" I asked.

" My dad. He's so uptight about everything. He smothers me and doesn't give me any flexibility. I just feel stuck. But I know what to do about it."

" Yeah, what?" I said a little love-drunk.

" We can sneak off. We can get to know each other a little and see where it goes from there. It's not just that I want to get out of the house. I also just want to get to know someone ... you know ... like a relationship or something. Do you think it's fate that we met?"

" Uh-huh," I said as I nodded.

But then I came to my senses.

" Well, uhum ..." I said in a lower voice. "It could be, but we won't know until we actually hang out a little, will we?"

" Exactly. So let's leave, now," she said quickly.

" Right now? Well ..."

" Do you have anything better to do?"

" No, it's not that," I said.

" Then let's go," she said.

" Wait. Let me tell my father."

" Oh, he'll discover it sometime. He does not mind, does he?"

" I guess not."

I still went to the bathroom door and knocked.

" What? I'm on the toilet, you shellfish!" he said in an irritated voice.

" I am going around the block. You can just leave without me. I'll be back around 9:00 p.m." I said.

" Sure. Do whatever you like. Stay out of trouble."

When we were out, we ran into a guy with glasses, not sunglasses this time but regular ones. His suit was black and his shoes were brown. He had a lisp and seemed like one of those frightening characters in a movie.

" And where are you both going?" he asked.

" Nowhere really," I said. "Just walking in the garden."

" Doesss the bosss know about thisss?" he asked.

" Yeah, he knows about it," I lied.

We got out of there as quickly as we could ... didn't even use the front door but snuck through the window, as suggested by Cynthia. When we were outside the front gate of the huge villa, she showed me her car. It was a Porsche.

" Wow, great car," I said.

" Yeah, I guess. It's actually expensive, but I never get to use it. I'm not into all that luxury stuff," she said. "But what I want, is to check out the world and to actually have someone that cares about me."

" I see what you mean. Your dad has been smothering you, hasn't he?"

" Yes. See? You are wise. I like you. You get me."

" What about the Missis?" I asked.

" My mom passed away five years ago," she said.

" Sorry to hear that. Where do you want to go? Shall we head out to eat?"

" Great idea. Yes."

" And what type of food? Italian?"

" Ah, no, no, no ... I always eat Italian. Are you insane?"

" I was just kidding. How about Peruvian?"

" I never had sushi," she said.

" Then sushi it is. Can I drive you there?"

" Be my guest."

GOOD! I was so loving this! I was driving a sports car with the best looking girl I had ever met right next to me. I jumped in and had a smile on my face. I turned the key, switched the gears, and hit the gas.

Vrooom!

This car was so insanely fast! I was certain it hit the speed of light. Well, perhaps not, but still ... it was actually fast. But something wasn't right. It was like someone was following me. I didn't comprehend at the time how someone could follow a sports car this fast, but perhaps my pursuer had a sports car too. I didn't mention it to Cynthia though, since I didn't want her to be worried.

We drove until we reached a Japanese restaurant. It was a pretty place, with designs and trendy ornaments on the door and asian things in the interior. We took a seat as guided by the waiter, and we took the menu.

" So many choices," Cynthia said. "I love this place already. It makes you really think that you're in a different world."

We talked for almost an hour. It was a lovely night and we had a fun time. I came to find out about her passion for music and dancing, and we talked about life in the gang. She mentioned she had always wanted to get out of it anyway, that she wanted to become a sincere person.

After a while, though, I noticed the same guy with the black suit we met in the corridor earlier. What was he doing in this restaurant? Had he been following us here? It made me suspicious.

I didn't trust that guy with the glasses and the black suit in the first place. I knew he was going to do something, specifically when I saw him being in the same restaurant at a different table.

I got up and saw him get up at the same time. This wasn't leading to anything great. I just had a hunch. It was too much of a coincidence. Then I saw him pulling a weapon from his suit. He was pointing it directly at me. Thankfully, I saw it in time and jumped down on the floor.

" What are you doing?" Cynthia asked.

Bang!

A shot echoed through the air. No one got hit, but everybody stressed out. People screamed; they all left the restaurant, including the waiters. Cynthia dove on the floor, beside me. I signaled to her to be silent. She was shivering, since she was extremely scared.

The guy with the glasses walked towards me, but he could not see me because of all the tables, chairs, and tablecloths. When he came really close, I jumped up and hit the gun out of his hand.

A hand-on-hand combat followed after that. He kicked me to the ground, punched me in the face, and elbowed me in the ribs. I think he threw a few good punches, but I still had my pride. I didn't think any person had to help out at that moment. I was doing fine, wasn't I?

" Ughhh ..."

Another hit.

" Ouch!"

Another punch.

This guy was pounding on me! He was undoubtedly more competent when it came to sparring and street battles. I was vulnerable, lying on the floor and attempting to block his punches, but failing miserably and expecting a miracle. He started choking me with his firm grip around my neck, but then ...

BAM!

Something hit him on the head, because he dropped in front of me ... well, on me actually, after which I pushed him off me. He was knocked out by someone. When I looked up, I saw Cynthia standing there with a rolling pin in her one hand and her other hand on her hip. She stood there with attitude, as if she were trying to tell the guy to keep his hands off her man.

" Thank you," I said a little ashamed that I could not secure her.

" I know, I know," she said. "It does not feel good to be saved by a girl, does it? But all I did, was getting a weapon from the kitchen. That's the only way I could have knocked him out. You are still my knight in shining armor. Mmm ... I think this is going to be my favorite weapon," she said with a smile.

" Why was he trying to kill me?"

" Because my dad does not trust you," she said laconically. "I expected it."

" We need to tell my dad about this," I said.

" I concur."

We called the police and left before they got there, leaving the knocked out individual to their judgment and the Japanese employees as witnesses. Then we drove straight to my dad.

" Dad," I said as I barged into our home.

" What's going on, boy?" he asked.

" We need to quit this business, dad," I said.

" What are you thinking? We've been in this for a long period of time, kid. Why would you want to quit now? It's great money."

" I know, but one of Antoni's men just tried to kill me."

" Wait a minute," my dad said. "What did you do? Steal his furnishings?"

" Worse," Cynthia said as she walked in. "He took his daughter."

" Oh come on, son. Aren't there enough pretty girls out there? Why did you have to go after this one?"

" We only went on one date, dad!" I said. I was really upset. "Don't you see how crazy this is getting? Don't you think we can make our money in better ways? Before you know it, we're all dead! And now Antoni has his men sent out after me because I just dated his daughter ... once!"

" It is getting a little out of hand," my dad said. "But I have to go back in a few minutes anyway to drop off the golden apple."

" Fine, but bring a gun," I said. "I don't trust that guy for one bit."

No sooner said than done, we drove towards Antoni's mansion. Cynthia remained at our place, awaiting whatever was going to take place. She had disagreed with her dad's life style for so long that I even wondered if she would be upset if he would get killed. Time would tell ...

The guard was gone. He had disappeared, so we just knocked and entered the mansion.

We walked up the stairs and observed that it was terribly quiet in there. Where did everyone go? The door to the big boss' room was on the other side of the room. The 2 of us walked towards it and went inside.

Bang!

Before we knew it, Antoni shot my dad in the chest.

" Aaaarrghh!" he screamed in anguish.

Antoni laughed. "Ha-ha! You idiot! You though you could trick me, kidnapping my daughter and bringing a weapon in the house? You don't know who you're dealing with."

But I had a weapon too, and Antoni hadn't thought of that. Another shot echoed through the room.

Bang!

Antoni was shot through the head, due to my many hours of training. I was a sharpshooter, and I was extremely happy with it, particularly at that moment.

" Bye, bye, Antoni," I said.

" S-son," my dad said as he was attempting to say something, lying on the floor.

" Dad! Dad, please stay alive. I can call an ambulance and they can help you. Here, I'll get the phone now."

" Forget it, boy."

" But why?" I asked.

" When they see I am here, they will begin some kind of investigation, which will more than likely be the end of my life, because they will toss me into jail. There is absolutely nothing we can do. This is where I'll die. It's all right."

" No! It's not! You still have a way to change. You can't go now!"

He rolled over a little, to his side.

Hey, what was that?

Something fell out of his pocket.

It was the glowing golden apple. I decided to pick it up and noticed that it was tender. Maybe it could be eaten, although that would be unusual: Eating a golden apple with a purple glow.

Nonetheless, I had absolutely nothing to lose. My dad was going to die here anyway, so I might just see if this apple had any effect on him. I offered him a bite and got it. He took a bite from the apple and let his head drop on the floor.

Nothing at all.

How terrible.

But wait ...

Suddenly, my dad woke up. He looked energized. He got up and his wound was gone. He looked at me with big eyes. Then he looked at the apple.

With a dynamic voice, he suddenly said, "What sort of apple is that?"

" Well, it's the golden one," I said. "I thought it may have had some magical impact."

" Give me that!" he said as he snatched it from my hand.

He ate and ate till the entire apple was gone. Then he turned to me and said, "I feel great! Wow! It's like absolutely nothing happened at all!"

" But something did happen, dad. We nearly got murdered. This organization is a mess. We need to get outta here."

" You're right, son. I should have listened to you. Get your girlie and we'll leave town as quick as we can."

And so we did.

We went home, informed Cynthia of the shooting, grabbed our valuables, and left the city ... in the Porsche, obviously. Cynthia was happy to come with us. The loss of her dad wasn't as intense as I expected it to be.

We moved to the other side of the country, far from the anguish and the corruption of the mob. We sold the Porsche and bought a small home. The old home got sold within months, but nobody was able to track us down.

And Cynthia and I? Let's just say that she had some attachment concerns to conquer, since her dad had squeezed the soap so much and controlled her too much. But after a little therapy, she ended up being freer and felt better every week. We talked a lot; we dated a lot, and eventually, we got married. It was the better life.

THE END

Printed in Great Britain
by Amazon